Scattershot

Collected Fictions

I0678647

Scattershot

Collected Fictions

Amy L. Eggert

ISBN: 978-1-943170-00-5

Cover Design: Jane L. Carman
Interior Design: Jessica Smith
Production Director: Jane L. Carman

Primary Typefaces: Baskerville and Onyx
Other Typefaces: Marker Felt, Courier New, Monotype Corsiva, Zapfino, and Engravers MT

Published by: Lit Fest Press, Carman, 688 Knox Road 900 North, Gilson, Illinois 61436

festivalwriter.org

for Ross

Table of Contents

Scattershot

In a flash of light off steel,
the boy turned into a man,
paralyzed at the threshold,
not yet thirteen,
his sweaty palm locked in
the girl's two-fisted grip.
She cowered in his shadow,
an ashen wraith in a My Little
Pony nightgown. Across
the room, their mother shrugged
against the stove, the blade
quivering in her hands, her
left eye puffed and purpling,
swollen from rage or a surprise
right hook. A stripe of red
straddled the Man's forearm,
droplets of blood drizzling
on kitchen tile.

The Man thundered something about forgiveness, something about
adverse effects of the medication, something about show some
fucking compassion, something about an exaggerated startle
response, something about snapping her neck like a twig.

The pair in the doorway ignored
or unseen, ghost children caught
in the periphery but lost
when given full attention.

The Man died dangling from attic rafters, a rope snaking ceiling-
down, coiled around his neck.

When the boy was in grade
school, a neighborhood block
party exposed him to what
their mother called post-
traumatic stress disorder.
Purple popsicle juice melted
over his fingers as he watched
the Man flip over the snack
table when the high-schooler
next door set off the firecrackers.
Smaller kids snickered as parents
pulled them off to the side,
as corn cobs bounced off
the sidewalk, as potato salad
littered the lawn. The Man
huddled behind a card table,
color draining from his face,
tears streaming like a child's
from pinched shut eyes,
knees of his jeans stained red
in a puddle of punch.
Picnic trench warfare.

The Man lost his leg in a roadside bomb explosion in Iraq. In the same
moment, he watched his friend blown apart, from the waist up: gone.

The boy would waken
to the sound of thunder.
In a window flash of lightning,
the Man would appear,
his silhouette black against
purple sky, his back to

the boy, staring inarticulate
out into the night. In the next
flash of light, the pane
would be empty, shade
framing drops of rain
splashing off the outside,
the boy wondering whether
he'd been dreaming, asleep.
Sometimes in the next room,
the Man's voice, the low-
pitched rumble of distant
gunfire.

The Man died mistaken as an intruder, a baseball bat to the skull.

The Man was a residual
haunt in the house, moving
as a shadow through hall
ways, walls, his daily routine.
Unaffected by those around
him, a storm passing through.
The night he returned, crownless
and on crutches, their mother
whispered something about chronic nightmares and flashbacks, a
bout clinical depression, about patience, leeway, the need for space.

The highs of combat
were unattainable in civilian
life, so the Man sought them
in what others deemed reckless
behavior, in bar brawls and
bottles of scotch discarded
in bulk in the garage, under
the kitchen table, on the back
porch, in the purr of his black
Honda Shadow Spirit.

The popping, snapping of cartilage, of tendons letting go,
the splintering of bone. The Man knew his leg was gone
as soon as the shrapnel chewed into his flesh.

The Man died flying back into battle, the engine sputtering, failing, a shining speck in the sky, plunging.

The girl's adolescence
was marred by pink tufts
of insulation wafting,
recollections of kitchen
knives glinting in the light,
blood trickling onto tile,
her fear reflected in their
mother's eyes, and
hopscotch on the rocks
paper scissor.
She sank.
The boy's own strange
and phantom fury matured
alongside stacked firewood
and slurred accusations.

Something about that girl shows no respect, something about teach your goddamn kids some goddamn manners, something about don't make me take matters into my own hands, 'cuz so help me god I'll do it.

The girl came home one
morning, a baby inside, left
with a split lip and their mother,
came home again, a stitched lip,
the baby gone.

The Man lost his leg to a motorcycle accident between tours, asphalt tearing, ravaging his flesh like shrapnel. The popping, snapping, letting go. The splintering of bone.

The Man died at seventeen, crossing the street toward an arcade, drunken high beams swerving.

The boy was the ghost
in the house, the phantom
warrior turning furious,

the fear of turning into the Man,
rage scaling his throat like bile,
too acidic to contain, white
phosphorous daydreams
of his father, the Man,
towering over the mangled
faces of disfigured children,
their bulbous features rotting
off in hospitals where injured
soldiers cried for their mothers.

The Man died at 86, a leg lost to diabetes, heart stuttering, failing.

Their mother screamed at the Man
once, charged him with being
insensitive, inaccessible,
abusive, abrasive, amputated
from her, from their children,
from responsibility, from reality.

The Man snatched his shotgun
from its dusty mount on the wall.
Drunk on adrenaline, on scotch
on the rocks, on antidepressants,
on blue sleeping pills, bombed
out of his mind, out of his left
boot, his buddy blown in half,
he warned her to back off,
to stand down, or he'd blast her
head off, he swore to god.
Still she charged, her voice
the shrill siren of an inbound
air raid.

The girl's hands over her ears,
the boy wrested the 12 gauge
from the Man's grip, wrestled
him to the floor, but not before
shells exploded at close range,
insulation snowing down

from the ceiling, pink confetti
flecking the family room carpet,
ears left ringing, a jagged drywall
patch, a painted-over scar,
a reminder, a token, a souvenir
from battle on the home front.

The Man died in a pool of blood and body parts, debris on a dusty
street in Fallujah.

The Man often disappeared
in the middle of the night
in a flash of lightning
through bedroom curtains,
in a fluorescent wink off
a steel blade, in the chink
of ice on glass, in a motorcycle
snarl. Most mornings he
returned, hobbling on
a hangover or a prosthetic leg;
on others, at the kitchen
counter, their mother nursed
a cup of coffee, black, sipping
slowly, watching the back door,
listening for the distant wail
of sirens or tires screaming
over wet blacktop, waiting
for the apologetic knock
of tragic news brought by
the pair of disheartened
though stoic police officers
who hated this part of the job
until finally splashing the cold
remnants into the sink, retreating
to the back corners of the house
in silence.

Sometimes before the shower
shut off, the boy could hear
through his bedroom wall

their mother weeping beneath
the white noise of water
hitting her.

The Man lost his leg to a drunk driver as a teenager and even
into his fifties complained of phantom limb pain, sensations
of tingling, itching, burning, aching in his missing left ankle.

Before pink flurries
and threshold paralysis
transformed the boy phantom
furious, he climbed attic stairs
in search of tangled strands
of Christmas lights, found
instead the Man, his throat
bruising purple inside a knotted
noose, lips trembling in dread
or prayer, his eyes wide
and afraid. The boy cut the rope
loose with a slip joint pocketknife,
held his father's hand as the Man
inched rung by rung back down
off the ladder. Together they
strung the flashing colored bulbs
along the gutter.

The Man died in the road, flesh fused to metal and asphalt.

One chilled afternoon, the Man
chopped, the boy stacked
firewood. The sky, the lawn
decorated with the red and orange
and gold of autumn leaves.
They worked in the backyard
where the Man had taught
the boy how to balance the log
and arc the ax, how to watch
the ball and swing the bat
parallel to the ground while
the girl stooped nearby,

scrawling purple hearts
and hopscotch squares
with sidewalk chalk onto
the concrete patio slab.
The boy steadied a branch
between gloved hands, cracked
it in two.

The sudden fracture of wood,
the unexpected rupture of grain,
the family tree: the splintering
of bone, the concussion of riflefire,
the snapping of a wife's neck.
The Man turned on his son,
ax suspended over his head.

Leaves unleashed, letting go
of the trees, floating wearily
from the sky, bloody, like scraps
of heaven falling, like drops
of blood raining to kitchen tile,
like tufts of pink dropping
from holes in the family
room ceiling, like snow.

The Man died mangled on the kitchen floor, blood spreading black
beneath him on the tile.

The visitation was closed
casket so as not to showcase
the rope burns, the purple
shrapnel scars, the third degree
road rash, the dented forehead.
The Man's flag-draped coffin,
the organ prelude, the candlelit
shadowflickers against stained
glass, the boy's somber
and straight-faced eulogy,
the girl clutching to their mother,
the soldiers' 21 gun scotch shot

salute, the folding over of striped
and starred cloth, the sinking
of the Man's remains into soft
earth, the quiet retreat of three
home to a haunted house.

Listening for limped footfalls
on concrete outside, the chill
of aluminum in a sweaty palm,
the boy was the specter unseen,
the shadowed sentinel behind
the refrigerator, waiting.
The Man's staggered entrance,
keys fumbling, cursing inarticulate
under whiskey breath, his sword
of Damocles in the guise
of a baseball bat
locked in the boy's two-
fisted grip.

Into Ruin

Somewhere a baby screams, and this is what stirs him, blinking, from blackness, a ten-year-old boy who clutches a woman's purse to his chest. He is lying on grass. A briefcase cushions his face. Sunlight glitters off splinters of glass in his hair and on his clothes, the blades around him flecked with it. He sits up slowly, blinks.

In one direction, sunshine slices through rolling white clouds; in the other, smoke darkens the sky, black and billowing. He stands, nearly stumbles over a jagged shard of metal as big as his bike. Hugging the purse, he moves slowly toward the sounds of the screaming baby. As he walks, the scene smooths into focus, and this is when he hears the other sounds.

Women wailing. Far away sirens. One man curses, a long loud string of obscenities he barks over and over and over. The rapid *ding-ding-ding-ding* of the crossing gates with their pulsing red bulbs. Someone coughs and coughs. Two little girls hold each other and shriek for their daddy. Flames crackle and spit sparks skyward. Lost inside all of this, the infant, nowhere to be seen, won't stop crying, can't.

Without checking for traffic, the boy steps off a curb onto a street, his ankles and knees shaking.

A man hewn in half bleeds out onto concrete, his torso and arms shuddering violently, his eyes wide, searching the sky. Two women hobble past him, don't seem to see him, one with a deep gash in her calf, the other dirty and dazed, shouldering the injured one's weight. Limbs without bodies twitch on the ground. Some are hands with wedding bands or nail polish. Some are feet still wearing socks and shoes. A small crowd of men and women, all wet from sweat and blood, tear into wreckage, pry metal away and pass heavy handfuls to people behind them who pass to the people behind them and so on. A little boy or girl lays face-down in the ballast, the leg of a stuffed bear locked in his fist, in her fist. A woman with white hair bends low over a man on his back. His own white head rotates from side to side as though he disagrees with something she is saying. His legs are buried beneath a reflective wall of windows. She clasps his hands inside hers. Train cars, fractured, cracked open, twisted and overturned snake away from the tracks. Already the flies buzz in swarms.

The boy takes all of this in and moves on, into the smoke and ravaged remains and the ruins, still clutching onto the purse.

Return to Summer

Arriving home, I find myself in an unfamiliar place; everything has changed. What I remember to be a pair of ponds divided by a slow two-lane residential overpass is now a set of parking lots flanking a four-lane high-speed route between shopping centers and office buildings. A bike path I remember snaking through the forest preserve now veers in a different direction, away from the trees. The used bookstore where I traded lemonade stand earnings for bargain paperbacks is now an organic foods market holding outdoor rummage sales on Saturday mornings. The cul-de-sac across the street is a vacant, browning lot where a man wearing leather stares at nothing and smokes his cigarettes.

The mailbox at the curb of our property that I remember encircled by tangles of hostas and daffodils is now affixed to the side of the house by the front door, a black metallic envelope that clangs open and shut. And of course the in-ground pool in the backyard, too-blue water shimmering white under sunlight, now filled in with crushed rock and sand and dirt and topsoil, and still nothing grows there.

Even the weather seems somehow changed; the warm summer sky of fragrant breezes through screens has given way to the harsh light of a slate gray sky, a stagnant sort of mildew smell in the air, and it's June.

I agreed to stay with my parents for a few weeks, an indeterminate amount of time, however long was necessary to move granddad into an assisted living facility, to organize and clean his house, to paint it and get it on the market, to find and insure that his end-of-life documents are in order and properly prepared for the inevitable—not because I know how to deal with these kinds of things, but because I was willing, and because my parents are overwhelmed with the process.

Hanging up with my mother that evening in April after we'd made the decision—she'd started to cry, out of exhaustion, gratitude—I couldn't help but resent my brother for not helping out with any of this, for leaving it to me to ease their anxieties, to stamp out any familial fires that sparked to life.

But I knew it wasn't fair to resent him; after all, I offered to help. This was my decision. And in the weeks leading up to the visit of unstipulated duration, I struggled not to think of my brother at all, even though the more I resisted, the more I conjured up those thoughts, and to think of summer at all was to think of my brother and vice-versa, and I couldn't shake the image of his lazy, impassive gaze as the rest of us around him smoldered into a frenzied panic. So I alternated between resentment and guilt over that resentment, and I wanted so badly for him to know how angry and abandoned I felt but not to tell him.

I want to feel nostalgic as I pull into the driveway, past the place where the mailbox and the hostas and the daffodils were once rooted. I think about my brother soaping the hood of our father's sedan with a dripping sponge, gray water streaming into the street. I push the thought away, can't feel that tug of reminiscence, of longing for what was. Instead I feel a numb tingling in my fingers, a pang of paranoia as I climb from my car and the man across the street flicks a cigarette away, lights another one and stares, a fluttering dread at finding the mailbox affixed to the side of the house.

"So much to do," my mother hugs me, says, instead of saying hello. And right away we're sorting through papers and she's telling me about the intake meeting at the assisted living facility that did not go well, and she's directing my father to carry my bags back to my old bedroom, "unless you'd rather stay in Brian's room," she says, and I say my old bedroom is fine.

This is how I end up lying in my old twin bed, between sheets as old as me, and I watch the ceiling while my parents sleep, frantic trapezoids of light darting across the room as passing headlights refract through the smeared windowpane.

Granddad is my only surviving grandparent. The other three died before I was old enough to mourn the loss of them, though I recognized grief caused by their deaths in those around me. When her own mother died, my mother retreated to her station wagon in the dark garage, sat in the driver's seat with the windows rolled up, and played a Patsy Cline cassette for hours every day until the tape wore out. She didn't speak or sing along or cry, just stared straight ahead through the windshield at the frayed lawn chairs dangling from nails on the garage wall. Some days my brother and I would climb into the backseat and listen with her.

When my father's parents died in a bus accident, my father pitched our rotary phone into the kitchen window—receiver, cradle, and all—shattering the glass. If not for the cord that tethered it to the kitchen wall, I imagine we'd have had to fish the phone out of the swimming pool in the backyard. Then he sank to the floor and wept.

As we drive toward the assisted living apartment complex, my mother warns me not to bring up granddad's house or the repairs we've been orchestrating. "He's devastated," she tells me. "And he wants to go home. Seems not to hear me when I tell him he has to stay put." My father clears his throat from the backseat. She goes on, "It's hard to blame him; he doesn't fit in there, you know. His mind is still there, but his body's failing him. We couldn't just leave him in that big house all alone to fall down those stairs or slip in the shower, or what if there was a fire? What would he do if there was a fire?" "We did the right thing, Mom." I watch houses slide past my window.

"It's just so sad to see him feeling like an outsider. It's like when your dad and I first started going to group. Everyone tried to sympathize with our situation, but, it wasn't the same. We didn't lose our child, so it was different—" "Like hell it was," my father snaps. "No, honey, it was. It was different…"

I squirm under my seatbelt. To change the subject, I ask about the mailbox, why the switch, mention how the green and yellow at the curb always let me know I was coming home. "What mailbox?" My mother swerves to avoid a squirrel in the road.

Granddad watches a muted soap opera from a plastic-covered chair. His walker lies shoved onto its side by his feet, looking like a snubbed pet. "Dad, look who's here to see your new apartment." He ignores my mother as she squeezes his shoulders from behind. I crouch to his side, kiss his cheek, say, "Hi, Granddad," which collects his attention. "Hello, sweetheart," and he takes my face in both of his wrinkled and shaking palms. "Are you here to take me home?"

At night I watch the spastic patches of light scurry across the ceiling. Thoughts crowd around me, and I'm frightened by their bulk, by the way they chase and crash into each other without any space or breath or punctuation between. My brother cupping his hands over mine, careful not to release the captured, flashing firefly. Grandad's trembling touch. My father's gravid silence from the backseat. I try to push the thoughts away, but they keep accumulating, stacks of cardboard boxes of childhood things packed and too many to be stashed away. A loud pop springs me away, up from my old twin bed and toward the window that faces traffic. The cars that creep past move with an under-water quality through the smeared pane, like they're pushing through undercurrents. I have to remind myself that this is not the city where I've been living for the past twelve years. Every abrupt blast is not a gunshot. In this suburbia-turned-shoptopia, strange noises afterhours were most likely cars backfiring, raccoons toppling garbage cans, kids rocketing fireworks into the night sky from cul-de-sacs and empty parking lots. I remember scanning our street in both directions, nodding the go-ahead to my brother who lit the short fuse with our father's zippo before we both bounded up our driveway, spinning around in time to watch pink sparks explode. I push the thought away, lie back down in bed, try not to think of my brother, watch the light on the ceiling.

Without thinking about it, I pick at paint dried on my fingernails.

Between coats, my mother meets with a lawyer about some of granddad's paperwork, and I pick up some lunch and drive to where the fishponds used to be. At my parents' house, I know my father is watering the oval deadspot in the yard that was an in-ground pool where nothing will grow. I know his jaw is locked in a scowl as he spreads more grass seed, as he jets more hose water over barren earth. I know that he lets the nozzle slip through his fingers to land on the ground, water spilling into the dirt, that he lets it lie there, a puddle spreading away from him. I know this because when I stopped there to deliver a sandwich, I saw him through the window. I left his lunch on the kitchen table and drove away, toward this place I remember that no longer exists.

Traffic zooms past in both directions, drivers impatient, honking at each other. I choose a bench at the edge of a parking lot that was a pond, and I toss scraps of crust onto the asphalt where I used to feed ducks.

Back at granddad's, we pull paint brushes out of the freezer, a trick my mother picked up from some home and garden television program, and get back to work. She sweeps a second coat of white onto the living room wall, and I tape off the trim in the adjoining kitchen. Drop-cloths drape furniture we've crowded into the middle of the room, sofas and lamps, jutting end tables. We walk on paint-spattered bed sheets, some I recognize as having belonged to Brian as a child, fire trucks and surf boards in primary colors.

Out of nowhere, she asks me if I've gone to see my brother recently. I change the subject, ask her to pass me a new roll of masking tape. "You've got time off; you should visit him." A renewed current of resentment, followed by guilt washes over me, and I will the emotions away, the ever-ebbing tide. "Brian doesn't care if I visit him," I say, disliking the slight whine in my voice. She hands me a wrapped roll of tape, looks at me. Her paint roller drizzles white onto a yellow surf board. "Honey, that's not true." I avoid her gaze, tear open the plastic and scratch at the tape, spinning the roll in my hands, searching for the cut edge.

For two weeks, every morning, I've been following dirt tracks into the woods, hoping to find remnants of the old bike path, but the trails always lead back out of the trees, back to the blacktop which leads away from the forest, away from underbrush and thick tree trunks that must have always been there, and I just can't remember where we used to ride, Brian and me racing, flying on our bicycles, air and sharp branches tearing at our windbreakers, our arms, the sky over our heads lost in leaves, our legs pumping, pedaling so fast we couldn't stop even if we wanted to, which we never did.

We get a phone call from the assisted living facility. Granddad is having some sort of episode, they say, and could one of us drive over to help calm him down. I volunteer; I convince my parents to let me go alone since he still seems to bear a grudge toward them for having left him there.

When I reach his apartment, I find two nurses in scrubs keeping their distance from him, hands raised in front of their chests as though to show they bear no weapons and intend him no harm. Granddad has stripped down to a bleached pair of boxers and clutches his walker with one knotted fist. His other hand jabs a gnarled finger in accusation at the women, and he is shouting.

"Bring me my clothes! I want my goddamn clothes!"

The women speak in soothing tones, taking turns, assuring him that they haven't got his clothes. But he shouts on.

I hurry to him, position myself between his walker and the women so that he has to focus on me. "Granddad? Granddad, what's wrong? Where are your clothes? What's going on?" His cheeks, I see, are damp with tears. His naked chest, skeletal and pale, heaves with each angry breath. "Granddad, where are your clothes?" But his eyes lurch away from mine, and he glares at the nurses standing behind me. I spin to face them. "Where are his clothes?"

One of the women leads me into his bedroom, to his dresser where one drawer juts askew, a handful of socks a heap on the floor, a pair of pants crumpled in the corner. I pull open a second drawer, find it full, pull open another, find it, too, is packed with clothes. I grab an undershirt, find the tag at the neck where my mother has printed granddad's initials with a marker. I carry it to him, hold it up for him to see. I struggle to keep my voice calm. "These are yours." He snatches the shirt from me and flings it to the floor. "My clothes are at home. I want my clothes! I want to go home!" Again, he's glaring at the women across the room, and I have to adjust my stance to block them from his view.

"Granddad, I want you to listen to me." I take his face in my hands, the same way he held mine on my first day back in town, and I find his eyes. "This, this place is home now." He clutches his walker. His shoulders sag a bit. "This is home now."

I'm afraid he's going to fall because his knees buckle and he wilts forward, and one of the nurses steps up to help me guide him to the plastic-covered chair in front of the television set. And I think of chlorinated water splashing. A reckless teenaged dare. My granddad's hands are shaking, and I think of Brian shaking, his lips bruising blue. And one of the nurses fills a glass with tap water and slides it into granddad's fingers and urges him to drink, drink it down, and I push my brother from my mind, but still he bobs to the surface, lifeless but alive, and I think of his deadpan gaze and his inability to talk or to tie his own shoelaces. And granddad lets the glass slip from his fingers like my father let the hose slip to the grassless ground, and it shatters on hardwood like chlorinated water splashing like a phone smashing a windowpane like a skull on the side of a pool, and he cries and grabs onto my hand, and we're shaking, both of us are shaking. And he pulls me closer to him, and he whispers into my face, "This isn't home, sweetheart. This isn't home."

Brick

Even the kind gestures—holding a door, the perfunctory well-wishing toward a day's work, the emptied dishwasher—all seemed to trigger animosity, to set one of them off the way fireworks can cast a combat veteran back into muddy, huddled trenches. The smoldering remains of a half-decade of cohabitation reignited only when the ash is stirred.

Even the cursory glance into an occupied room smelled faintly of lighter fluid.

He didn't believe she *hated* him. Well, sometimes, maybe, he did. She was young, after all, and he knew enough that young people possessed a ready urge to hate. Something he didn't understand but could almost remember.

Kane tapped the turn signal, used the opportunity of glancing in the rearview to steal a glimpse in Marie's direction. She peered out the passenger side window into early morning darkness, her hands folded primly in her lap.

Whispers overheard across her cousin's birthday party replayed themselves like scratchy cassette tapes in his mind. Her association with Kane she wore like a heavy medal of perseverance. One weighty enough to wilt her shoulders and cause her to sigh often. Readily broadcast around her family were a multitude of *We told you so; I'm surprised it's lasted* this *long; What did you expect going with a man so old?*; and a sprinkling of *Have you considered springing for a therapist?* The fact of the matter was that the prognosis of their sick non-nuptials was growing darker with each day.

The interstate stretched westward ahead, night's lightless sky an unending expanse of black; Kane sank lower into his seat. He let a long gust of air release from his lips. Beside him, Marie didn't twitch. He thought about twisting the radio knob, but knew no amount of white noise could surmount the bitter hush inside the car. Clearing his throat to hear something, he shifted uncomfortably beneath his seatbelt.

An oncoming truck's high beams doused them in yellow light, and Kane risked another furtive glimpse. Taut jaw muscles worked below smooth skin. Her eyes fastened to some unseen apparition out her window. Then the light was gone, and only her shadowed presence rejected him.

He sucked in a deep breath, held it. "Marie, I—"

The thunderous detonation flinched his head hard to the left; simultaneously he jerked the wheel. A sandlike spray gnawed through his right cheek.

Tires screamed, striping black rubber lines behind, 59 miles per hour to nothing as fast as his sole could pound the brake. Flung hard into the steering wheel, seat belt seizing his chest, Kane spun toward Marie cowering beneath an implosion of glass, most of it still hanging in spiderweb shards from the windshield, specks of it glittering in her hair, on her face, framed inside mosaic shadowlines.

A concrete patio brick collapsed her chest inward, spilled black-red from every corner.

Wild eyes rolled toward him. Her hands, still clasped like prayer in her lap, trembled. No voice slipped through her bloodied lips, only small gasps and sighs, her lungs crushed beneath the block.

Incoherent sputterings erupted from Kane's throat as he fumbled for her face with his palms. Helpless fingers shook, stroked her cheeks before groping for the seatbelt release at his own hip.

Leaning onto his door, he dropped out onto asphalt, hands first, crawling toward the front of the car. He heard Marie's labored breathing, gurgled gasps and sighs. His fingers clutched onto the car's front bumper, and without support from fear-numbed legs, he pulled himself to a crouch.

Overhead, the Broadway Bridge with its orange dome lights echoed Marie's wheezing pleas, his own panicked cries, and the resonance of two young boys laughing from the overpass and sprinting in the opposite direction.

II.

The skin stretched over Kane's knuckles is raw, scabbed over in places, shiny pink in others. Throughout the day, he flexes his fingers, bends them slowly, one after another, as if scaling invisible piano keys. He is doing this one evening while riding the bus. An aged woman seated across from him notices, pulls her purse strap closer to her body, shifts in her seat. Kane sees this but ignores it, flexes the fingers of his right hand, bends each one slowly, eases the stiffness away.

He knows what she must think of him, that at any moment that fickle spring of a conscience might snap inside his head, he might vault from his seat across the aisle and pounce on her without mercy, he might steal from her her meager pocket change, her address book, her life. Why? Because despite his fine clothes and posture, he is a ragged black man on a bus, his graying hair uncombed and untrimmed, his face unshaven, scarred on the right cheek, his knuckles raw, scabbed over in places, shiny pink in others. A time bomb with an unpredictable fuse.

Kane knows this, can see it in the way her eyes flit across and away from him, but he doesn't begrudge her for it. Before, he would have. Before, he would have begrudged and confronted her, calmly but with conviction, demanded that she acknowledge her groundless issues with him. But not now.

He is a ragged black man on a bus, even his hair standing up and away from him, unshaven, scarred face, raw, scabbed, shiny pink knuckles, and, as his father used to say, better the devil you know than the devil you don't.

Now accustomed to avoidance, both as the recipient and as the instigator, for the most part, Kane finds solace in the isolation. For the most part.

When the bus lurches to a stop, Kane watches the woman watch him as she carefully stands, her white knuckled fist grasping the strap of her purse, his knuckles, raw, scabbed, shining pink, flexing, scaling invisible piano keys. He could smile at her, offer some kind gesture, scatter some of her anxiety, settle the dread he knows is mounting inside her like steam off a rolling boil, like a crescendo, but he doesn't. Better the devil you know than the devil you don't.

Outside the bus' tinted windows, dusk appears darker than reality, but Kane knows by the rousing of headlights on cars, by the hurried gait of passersby, by the shadows lengthening over sidewalks and curbs that night is approaching. The bus pitches forward, and the few remaining passengers sway in their seats. Kane flexes his fingers, folds them into a fist, extends them again, bends them again.

His stop is coming.

The driver flips on a strip of overhead dome lights that flicker and buzz each time the bus bounces on its tires. Kane is miles from his home. He is unfamiliar with the street names on the signs that flash green past the windows of the bus, but he knows that his stop is coming. As the few straggling passengers disappear down the stepwell and onto dark sidewalks, Kane sits, notices the driver's eyes rise and meet his own in the mirror before darting away, back toward the end of the road. This is the avoidance Kane has grown accustomed to. A flash of acknowledgement, a swift retreat to seclusion. Before, Kane would have engaged the stranger in friendly conversation, a mundane exchange about the weather or the latest baseball standings, just to keep the other at ease. But not now.

Kane watches the world blur by out the windows, his own dark reflection staring him in the face, the flecked scars on his unshaven cheek tingling with each bounce of the bus, with each flicker and buzz of the dome lights overhead, and he watches the world outside, watches shadows stretch and lengthen, watches headlights pulse to life, watches pedestrians hurry toward hulking buildings, watches huddles of young people creep away from structures into the shadows, the streets, into the blackest parts of night. Kane watches them, the huddled packs of young people, of boys, flexes his fingers, his scarred cheek prickling, tingling.

He's on his feet before the bus brakes, before its bulk edges toward a curb to let him off. Inside his head, a fuse sparks, hisses. This is the tuneless music that accompanies Kane nightly as he steps off the bus, as his shoes hit pavement cracking to dust, sidewalks that wind as aimlessly into the dark as the young boys with their backs to him. Kane moves quickly, slips close to the buildings, the storefronts and diners with caged windows, the duplexes and multiplexes, the bars with their humming neon, the whore houses and crack houses; he merges into shadows. The boys with their backs to him huddle together, cuss and laugh. One of them kicks a beer bottle which shatters against his foot, shards of glass glinting under streetlights. The fuse hisses.

The skin stretched over Kane's knuckles is raw, scabbed over in places, shiny pink in others. He flexes his fingers, bends each one slowly, one after another, as if scaling invisible piano keys. Inside shadows, Kane, the fuse, the shrinking distance between Kane and the boys with their backs to him. The fuse hisses. Kane stalks them, folds his fingers into fists, his scarred cheek prickling, tingling, remembering a spray of hot glass.

Signs

Across the asphalt, the sign, proud and cardboard, staked between just blooming tulips in the garden behind the catholic church, angled toward traffic and toward the high school, catches her eye just like every afternoon as she sulks away from her campus toward her car, its big black block letters **Pray to End Abortion** leering, sneering, snaring her attention, her ire, and she wonders what the fuck, why the hell not **Pray to End *Causes* of Abortion** or **Pray to End Incest** and **Poverty** and **Damaged Baby Brains** and fucking **Date Rape**, like it's always some selfish kid using it as fucking birth control, like it truly is a fucking choice, like some earnest prayer or genuflection or signum crucis would suddenly make birthing a broken baby beautiful, and as she punches deep into her purse and tears her keys from inside, a man rounds the corner of the church, the priest with a watering can, and he meets her gaze, nods in greeting, so she thrusts her middle finger into the air, climbs into her car, and slams the door behind her.

Wings Off Flies

She wasn't crying anymore or whispering "Lola, Lola." She wasn't blinking anymore even though her eyes were looking at me. Her chest wasn't moving up and down up and down anymore. Her hand was still on my hand, but it didn't hold on anymore.

The students swiveled toward him. Callie Lewis stood at the front of the room gape-jawed, mid-sentence, her folder open in front of her. Dennis thumbed the switch on his stopwatch, glimpsing briefly down at the blinking digits.

"You know the drill." He jotted down Callie's time. "Wait for it."

The low whine wailing through the wall-mounted speaker ceased, and the students shifted their collective gaze back to the front of the classroom. A shrill pulse bleated its alarm.

"Tornado?" One of the students inquired.

"No, tornado is the long siren. This is fire."

"Fire is the bell. This is lockdown."

"Right, lockdown." Dennis closed his gradebook and stood. "Callie, since you are nearest the door, please make sure it's locked and hit the lights. Everyone, under desks."

A few of them snickered as they noisily shoved squeaking chairlegs across tile floor and clamored clumsily beneath desks smaller than themselves.

"Mr. Winchell, am I going to have to start all over?" Callie eyed him with repugnance as she palmed down the trio of light switches.

He half-smiled an apology and made his way, maze-like, around and between desks, chairs, and feet poking out from safe zones to his own desk.

"Put them away," he ordered toward various glow patches from cell phones he couldn't see. Accordingly, the patches vanished, and more muffled snickers ensued. The vertical rectangles straddling the door flashed white and black from the hallway strobes.

"Hey, fuck you, Zach, I got through almost half of it," Callie's voice rose from the shadows. More snickering.

Dennis Winchell squinted across the span of the room. As long as the assailant was deaf, the room could be taken for empty. He dropped into his chair and angled his oversized desk calendar toward the pulsating light. There at the top of today's date was a circled D in his scrawled green pen, scheduled for ten after two. Right on time. His eyes skated to the right.

The room flashed black. The room flashed white.

A low buzzing filled his ears. Breath stopped in his throat. A trickling chill emptied warmth from his face from the peak of his scalp to his stubbled chin. The agenda fragments—sub 1st period, 10:30 department meeting, exam period six, pick up dry cleaning—were unimportant. The number at the top left was what drained blood from his extremities. The eleventh. Jesus fucking Christ the eleventh. Tomorrow was the eleventh.

The room flashed. His vision swam red as he heaved open the top drawer and fumbled for the rattling bottle of pills. Alternating light blazed crimson, cherry, crimson, pulsed behind pinched shut eyes in tempo with throbbing temples and the screaming intercom.

```
I heard her breathing before I saw her. It sound-
ed bad, like she was sucking through a straw. But
like there was barely any juice left at the bottom
of the cup. She crawled to me, to my hiding place
under my bed. Her bathrobe was wet with blood. Her
throat was cut. I could see it shining black even
though the lights were off. She laid down next to
me like always when I had a bad dream. She squeezed
my hand in hers. It was hard for her to talk: "Don't
tell him." She was crying without making any sound.
```

Dennis swallowed three of the small pills with saliva alone, drew a deep breath. He struggled for air under red water, urged the drug to chase the bloody currents away.

He pictured his wife, fully clothed, hunched in an empty bathtub, hugging her knees, no sound, chest heaving, wracked with silent sobs.

The bursts of red faded to a dull brick. Dennis opened his eyes. The dark no longer strobed with intermittent light. He slipped pills four and five onto his tongue as the assistant dean came over the intercom with the all-clear announcement, congratulating the student body on a successful drill. He rose from his desk to flip the lights back on as his class bobbed and surfaced over desktops. He winced against abrupt fluorescent daylight.

"Callie? An encore?"

*

Something within Dennis' subconscious kept meticulous track of time. Though the calendar date caught him by surprise, a part of him sensed the impending anniversary with fervor. The nightmares had been increasingly vivid, intense and frequent. This week's feature positioned him in a familiar doorway, pumping his legs as hard as he could, yet as much effort as he exerted, he never moved an inch. He felt like one of the old Warner Brothers cartoons, legs a cyclical blur while his body remained fixed, poised for takeoff. However, unlike the animations, he was never propelled forward by that belated but invisible slingshot that left a plume of cloudy smoke in his wake. Instead, the threshold was ice, and his shoes slipped without progress for what felt like minutes. Behind him, his wife cowered on the floor, chipped fingernails clawing the wall, a creaturemoan spilling in anguish from her lips.

What worried him more than the nightmares themselves was when they transpired without sleep.

When his vision swam red. When all warmth drained from his face and settled into a molten knob of torrid dread in his throat. When he felt himself sinking deeper, deeper into dark water, limbs heavy, lifeless under the weight of it. When, late at night, sitting in his study with a stack of sophomore drafts, the steady drip, drip, drip echoed in his ears. When he followed the sound to the shadowed bathroom at the end of the hall, sweat pearling his forehead, hands pale and shaking, seeking out the switch plate on the wall. When, upon flipping the switch, his gaze inextricably crawled over dingy flooring, inched with growing trepidation, tile by tile, toward the brimming bathtub of blood.

Sometimes—not always—popping six or seven of those tiny white pills chased the scene away. More often, Dennis found himself crouching at the base of a dry tub, breathless and wet-faced, hands clutching helplessly at his chest.

*

His arrivals home were unembellished. A quiet unlocking and re-latching of the kitchen door, a cursory glance toward the lamplight deflected onto the hall carpeting toward the back of the house, and a hasty retreat to his study. Today wasn't different. The weight from his laptop case's strap gnawed at his shoulder, and he was eager to crack a beer, crank the sizable space heater in his study, and dive into the monotony of grading.

It was the monotony he clung to. His days were unchanging, fixed in their lackluster routine. No variation, no surprises. Not too many years before, he thrived more on the impulsive, less restrictive and more freewheeling with his time. Even at work, students often stopped him in the halls or at his office to chat, whether about an assignment, a college application, a troubling relationship issue, and he always made the time. Now he pulled out of his regular parking space at 4:15 exactly every afternoon, invited students with academic-related inquiries to shoot him an e-mail, pulled into his garage between 4:35 and 4:45 depending on traffic, quietly unlocked and re-latched the kitchen door, and ducked into his study.

Depositing gloves, scarf, and coat on a love seat just inside the door, Dennis paused at lamps throughout the room before landing at his desk. A mismatched pair of mugs, coffee staining the insides, awaited a trip to the dishwasher. Mounds of lined and printer paper stood in varying heights across the desktop, a sloppy skyline obstructing several silver-framed photographs. An out-of-place lavender sticky note was planted on the single exposed section of wood where his laptop slept at night.

Jaw locked, he read the two words scripted in his wife's recognizable cursive. With a conscious consideration of his blood pressure, Dennis balled the note in his fist and tossed it into the waste basket.

```
I couldn't hear him talking. I only heard her yell-
ing: "I won't tell you!" "You won't find her!" "I won't
tell you anything!" She screamed and then it sound-
ed like thunder crashing in the living room. Then I
heard plates and glasses and stuff breaking in the
kitchen. Heavy footsteps at my door. I thought he
was gonna find me. Then the footsteps stomped across
the hall into Mama's room. More stuff breaking.
```

"He sounded upset." His wife's voice startled him. As did her dark silhouette in his doorway. "Maybe you should go see him."

Dennis slumped into his chair and blew out a long, exasperated sigh. His gaze wandered past her without fixing on anything in particular, and without knowing it, he began shaking his head.

"Maybe it's time." Her voice was low and deliberate; it rarely rose above a murmur now, so unlike the bouncy, exuberant manner of not too many years before. She made no motion to step into the room. Shoulder propped against the doorframe, arms crossed firmly in front of her, she regarded him in silence.

He felt her eyes on his face, like tiny pinpricks on his flesh, and met her gaze.

"No." His own voice was barely audible. He cleared his throat, hoping to gather some vigor. "No. It's over. It's *been* over, it's—It's over."

She watched him, unblinking. He couldn't read her expression but knew she was drawing conclusions under that stone demeanor. She stood a moment longer, fixed in the doorway, unmoving, a staring match between husband and wife, before seceding. Her arms drooped lazily to her sides in a gesture of defeat, and she walked away.

"It's over," Dennis repeated to the empty room. Some strength had returned to his vocal chords, but still he was unsettled by the quiver under that last syllable. It was over; he felt resolute in that fact. It didn't matter how many phone calls or sticky notes, Dennis would not go see him. Too much had been lost. Too fucking much, and staring his older brother in the eye might loosen Dennis' already feeble grip on the near-composure he had fought so hard to wrap around his recently restructured life.

Alley Winchell was half the country away in a state penitentiary awaiting execution for killing two women. Dennis intended on keeping that distance between them. In fact, Dennis had not spoken to his brother since those ugly weeks of the trial, not since Alley's brooding face scowled from newspaper pages, websites, and newscasts, not since that January two years before, not since...

He sensed the red crowding toward his vision, starting at the periphery, buzzing, creeping inward, surging, its stranglehold clenching at his temples before washing over everything in sight. His limbs went numb. His pulse quickened. His throat closed as his lungs seemed to fill with that thick red liquid.

He groped at his empty pants pockets before scrabbling for the laptop case. The telltale rattle assured him he was close.

In his mind, he floated down the darkened hallway toward the bathroom at the end, slow-motion terror, legs pumping but struggling as if through sand, the door thrust open in a frame-by-frame to reveal the bloodwater, a pale arm, draped limp over the lip of the tub.

Seizing fingers wrenched the top off the orange prescription bottle, tilted an unknown number of its contents into a gaping mouth. He chased the medication with a cold splash of coffee from a day-old mug and clasped his face in trembling hands, praying to the tiny white angels on his tongue for some semblance of mercy.

After perhaps only seconds of desperate implorings and pleadings, the scarlet waters began to recede. His heart rate and breathing returned to normal, and a sickening prickling sensation bloomed in his fingers and toes, causing him to flex and extend until the tingling subsided.

```
She took a deep breath. I saw her shoulders move up
and she unlocked the door. "She isn't—" but that's all
she said before he pushed the door open so hard Grammy
fell down on the floor. She started to cry. I saw it was
him, and I ran back to my bedroom. I didn't want him to
see me there. I ran real quiet so he wouldn't hear me.
```

When he snapped to consciousness several hours later without realizing he had fallen asleep, Dennis was drenched in sweat and convinced he had been drowning in red water. He frantically pawed at his shirt and pants, searching for indicative stains. He found none.

In his apparent strugglings against the elusive dreamwater, he had scattered a stack of student papers from his desk, and they were strewn across the floor. As he bent to retrieve them, the crumpled purple sticky note caught his eye from the waste basket. Without sorting through the papers to make sure they were all same-side-up, he tossed the chaotic pile onto his desk and left his study for bed, not caring to switch lamps off.

*

His alarm sounded at exactly 6:30 as it did every morning. He carried a steaming mug to his desk and shuffled papers and folders into his bag. Stopping himself once, he reconsidered and retrieved the crumpled slip from the trash, smoothed it flat on his desktop. *Alton called.* Dennis drew a deep breath.

Alley's notoriety had begun at an inconvenient time in Dennis' life. Certainly no occasion was optimal to learn your brother had committed murder in the first degree, the murders of his girlfriend of three years and her mother no less, but the timing of the trial could not have been more problematic for Dennis and his small family. Dennis was up for tenure at the high school; his wife, too, was up for promotion at the hospital; and the media's connotation of the name Winchell cast shadows of trepidation over both employers.

But Dennis' self-imposed distancing from his brother began years before Alley had met the woman he would adore and asphyxiate. Alley was sullen and grudging, even as a child; the "mean streak" their mother diagnosed as a phase was one he would never outgrow. He bullied his classmates and his little brother, bending fingers back to cracking angles and imposing overpowering chokeholds that turned the boys' throats pink. He had been suspended from school fourteen times for starting (and winning) fights. He had been the sadistic adolescent who used to yank the wings off of flies, not to kill them, but to watch them writhe, helpless, in his palm, black thread legs curling as he cackled thunderously above.

Alley had frightened Dennis as a child, and truthfully, he frightened Dennis as an adult. As the televised trial updates headed in the direction of justice, Dennis breathed a sigh of relief, knowing Alley would get his "just deserts," a favorite adage of their mother before her death a decade prior. Still, he had accepted the occasional phone call and listened in silence without sympathy. Dennis had always reveled in the quiet resolve of knowing that, unlike Alley, he was a good man; he treated people with kindness, he was a law-abiding, god-loving citizen, and above all, he kept his family safe. He was the opposite of his brother in every regard, a protector to Alley's destroyer, a teacher to Alley's truant, a savior to Alley's beast, streaming sunlight to Alley's darkness.

Keeping track of the murder trial consumed his attention—his push for tenure, heading up the school's speech team, and daily teaching, grading, and conversing with students all vying for the same. He was consumed to the degree that when home, he didn't surface from his study until bedtime. Even meals were taken at his desk, watching the latest breaking news report, his brother's glower a menacing and prominent commercial tag that kept viewers tuned to the channel. He was consumed. And in his preoccupation, he failed to be aware of those closest to him.

Voices in his house faded into white noise. Family faded into shadows that darkened his threshold as they passed into other rooms. Ghosts.

Now his wife rattled dishes in the kitchen, collecting his attention back from the past. The faucet spilled into the sink. Dennis glanced through his doorway, but she was around the corner, out of sight. He considered calling to her, inviting her into his study, offering some small gesture of amity, but he could think of nothing to say. The same as every other day, they existed in the same house but at opposite ends, in separate spaces, and even when crossing paths, a quick joyless smile, sagging eye contact, a raising of eyebrows, the occasional obligatory questioning about a day's work. Neither seemed to care enough about what the other considered small talk, and to breach the topic that had silenced them in the first place seemed to Dennis too catastrophic to even contemplate. Even on this, the anniversary, the eleventh, he couldn't conjure the simplest of words to utter to his wife.

Dennis plucked hat, coat, and scarf from the love seat and slipped in silence out the kitchen door.

*

The sky, slate gray and etched with the hazy outlines of clouds, seemed to hover low over the cold ground as Dennis pulled up along the familiar fence line. No snow yet, but the temperature dipped to freezing, and Ice Possible kept flashing on his car's digital thermometer at the lower corner of his rearview mirror. As he braked, he half-anticipated the red to start swimming in from his periphery, and he eyed his laptop case slumped in the passenger seat, where his consolation, a bottle of white pills was safely tucked away. The surge didn't come. Dennis unbuckled his seatbelt but left the key in the ignition.

Through the windshield, tall gates to the cemetery stood open.

A quick glance at his watch assured him he still had a half hour before he needed to be back at work for second period. Plenty of time. And yet he hesitated, body and mind at war against each other, wanting to move and wanting simultaneously to stay put. He peered out over stones and gentle hills, bouquets of flowers barely discernible, small pockets of color standing out against the gray.

He fished his pills from his bag and forced open his door. The icy wind bit into his face, and he readjusted his scarf and hat so only his eyes were exposed. He shoved his gloved hands deep into his coat pockets. The entrance before him gaped, the wind at his back urging him forward. He stopped at the gates, taking in the burial plots of so many daughters and sons, parents and grandparents, soldiers and strangers. He thought of his mother, of visiting her grave with Alley, of Alley cursing and kicking at dandelions, chanting, "It just ain't right, buddy boy; it's not fuckin' right," chugging beer after beer from a six pack he had carried along, pacing, pitching empty cans onto neighboring plots. That had been eleven years ago, the rapid conclusion to a vicious onslaught of terminal cancer that withered their mother away in seven fast months. "It ain't fuckin' right."

Dennis couldn't go in. He knew he had to, that he owed her that much. But he couldn't. He couldn't will himself forward. Even today, on the anniversary, he couldn't take that first step.

A low buzzing filled his ears. His stomach lurched. He felt his pulse quicken, heard it join the buzzing in his ears. He winced against the wind and the budding red and hurried back toward the car, his fist locked around the pill bottle in his pocket.

Once safe in the warmth of the car, Dennis rifled through his bag, pried a sweating water bottle from inside and twisted the top off, chased white pills down his throat. His own pallor in the rearview alarmed him. Ice Possible engraved across his brow like a caption. He dabbed at his forehead with his gloved fingertips, tossed his hat to the floor. He returned to his bag in search of his handkerchief. A purple sticky note was wedged between papers, and he knew his wife must have planted it there just this morning.

He wants you to know that he's sorry...

Two years ago. It had been the same evening the woman stood in front of the Brookwood County courthouse wearing a fur bucket cap, snow spitting in fury around her face, and announced to the viewers at home that "Forty-one year old Alton Samuel Winchell was sentenced to death today, following a heated eighteen day trial, in which the heart-wrenching, eye-witness testimony of Lola Patton's nine-year-old son, Anthony, sealed the deal for jurors..."

Dennis had been clutching his hands so tightly together that they throbbed, his nose mere inches from the television screen, his knees stiff and aching from holding his crouch position. His wife had stood behind him, kneading his shoulders.

It had been the evening of his final conversation with his brother who had been allowed to phone from the courthouse before he was transported back to the penitentiary. "This is it, buddy boy," Alley had said. "It's over." And Dennis struggled for words of condolence, struggled to mean it, because as much as Alley frightened him, Alley was his brother, and Alley was going to die.

It had been the evening after his second tenure review meeting, and Dennis' anxiety level was high. The week before, his wife had been denied promotion. As he studied the apathetic and unimpressed faces of his colleagues, Dennis knew they followed the news, and he knew that, like him, they awaited the inevitable broadcast: his brother would be shipped to death row. All of this had weighed heavily on his mind that evening as he and his wife consoled each other on the love seat in his study, TV muted and lights off, sleet rapping steadily against the windowpanes.

Suddenly his wife had lifted her head from his shoulder. "Where's Abbie?"

"Haven't seen her," he had replied as his wife stood and stretched from sitting too long in one position. Dennis sulked in the rapid flashes of commercial light, vaguely heard her as she had moved from room to room, pulling open doors, calling Abbie's name, as she had knocked politely on the closed bathroom door.

Grammy flapped her hand in front of her, shooed me back toward the hallway like I was a fly buzzing in her face. Her voice was quiet but mad: "Get back in bed. Mind me, Anthony. Go on, now." She tied her bathrobe tight and put both hands on the door and looked through the peephole. Then her hand touched her chest like she was going to say the pledge. She turned back to the hallway but she didn't see me still standing in the shadows.

Dennis had spent the evening pitying himself and his murderous brother while his daughter bled out into bathwater, the steak knife she'd used to slice her own wrists sunken to the bottom of the tub. By the time he reached her, he had been too late. Dennis stood paralyzed on the threshold, both hands gripping the doorframe for support, his wife moaning and tearing her fingernails on the wall and carpet behind him, his seventeen-year-old daughter open-eyed and bathing in her own blood before him. He had been too late.

And every day Monday through Friday, nearly every hour, eight o'clock in the morning until three-twenty in the afternoon, a different dozen breathing reminders ambled into his classroom, sat slumped in plastic chairs, gawked up at him with thick-lashed blinking eyes and flushed cheeks, life and sarcasm and teenage rebellion coursing through pulsing, invigorated veins. At times he longed to reach out to one of them, smooth her hair, pull her into his waiting arms, but for a multitude of obvious reasons, he restrained himself, perhaps the foremost being he might not let go.

Instead, the bell rang to end the period, and he urged them to shoot him an e-mail with any questions.

Dennis pulled into his regular parking space and headed toward the school, displacing his thoughts of Alley, of Abbie with lecture notes for second period.

*

The classroom buzzed with pencils scratching paper; students hunched over their desks, uniform in their motionless concentration. Dennis stared, unseeing, at papers while his sixth period students poured over their exams. He meant to get some grading done, but his mind swam with two-year-old images: The bathtub of blood. Alley's brooding expression on the TV screen. The photocopied transcript of nine-year-old Anthony Patton's eyewitness testimony. His wife's chipped fingernails. Abbie's arm, limp and bloodless, flung over porcelain. His wife, fully clothed and moaning, mourning in the dry tub.

The moaning, the low whine wailing through speakers. It took Dennis a moment to realize the sound was not summoned from his recollected wife but from the front of the classroom. The students glanced in unison up from their exams. The initial warning halted, and Dennis waited with the rest for the distinct signal to alert the school of the emergency. The shrill pulse of the lockdown alarm sounded, and strobe lights flashed to life in the hallway.

The students turned toward Dennis as he fixed a calm expression over his features.

"You know what to do."

The students dropped pencils and shoved back in their chairs, disappearing one by one beneath their desks. Dennis stood, casting a quick glance down toward his calendar, checking for his scribbled shorthand. No circled D. He felt his heart hitch in his chest. This wasn't a scheduled drill.

He flipped the trio of switches down as the hallway fluorescents dimmed to black, the flash of the emergency strobes off, on, off, on. He swung the classroom door shut and peered out into shadows through the adjoining strip of glass.

Someone was banging on the front door. Not knocking like they wanted someone to answer, but banging like they were trying to get inside. Like it didn't matter if someone opened the door for them or not. Like it didn't matter if the door was locked.

Dennis shifted his gaze back toward his classroom, the empty desks. No one whispered or snickered. No one made a sound. He felt he should make an announcement, remind his students to remain calm, that things would be fine, that this was why there were drills, that they'd all come out of this after a few minutes. He wanted to promise them they'd survive. But he couldn't. There was nothing he could do. For these other parents' children, for his own child.

Dennis slumped against the door, the piercing alarm slamming at his temples. Something dark and sinister stalked their children, and he was helpless to stop it. Soundless students crouching under desks. A bathtub of blood. A small boy hiding under his bed clutching a dead woman's hand. Always returning to the moment of utter helplessness. Standing in the doorway, realizing what had happened. That she was dead. That no amount of chest or towel compressions could bring her back or stanch the flow of red from her wrists. That he had failed. He had been too late. There was nothing he could do. *He wants you to know that he's sorry about Abbie.* There would either be an all clear or there wouldn't. There was nothing for any of them to do but wait.

Parallel Play

"We can't keep him."

This was after Mrs. dabbed at eyes with damp tissue, Mr. beside her, staring into space, saying things like "doesn't get along" and "doesn't listen" and "done all we can."

This was after: "He hits."

This was after: "Please understand. I think Billy's acting out—"

This was after marker squeaked against paper. Angry red splotches. Small fist smeared, stained, shiny wet.

This was after: "Billy, wait out here" and "color a nice picture."

This was after: "nothing's physically wrong" and "he's four years old" and "why isn't he talking?"

This was after Billy, whimpering, pulling away, Mr.: "Come on, buddy, we have to go upstairs." Billy shaking his head, slumping to knees, Mr. stopping walking: "Billy, stand up. Don't make me carry you. You're a big boy; now stand *up!*" Billy snatching hand away, covering eyes. On his knees, spinning away from staircase. Mrs.: "God damn it, Paul, just pick him up." Mr. climbing stairs, Billy, thrashing, hiding eyes, wrapped tight in Mr.'s arms. A woman's voice from the landing:

"Sorry to get your message."

This was after: "That's it, Paul. I'm done."

This was after sharp slap to Billy's cheek. Mr.'s angry words: "This is not how we behave, Billy!"

This was after little girl screamed and screamed. Mrs. cradling her in close embrace, whispering words to soothe, but still the girl screamed. "Paul, I'm afraid it might be broken." Mr. snatching Billy's arm, dragging him away from staircase.

This was after: "No, Billy, that's *mine!*" Girl reaching for doll, nearly catching yellow yarn hair, Billy chucking it down stairs, watching wide-eyed, doll tumbling step after step. "Mean, Billy!" Little girl pushing past, Billy shoving her shoulder hard, little girl losing footing, rolling into sloppy somersaults, thud after thud until landing at bottom beside yellow yarn hair. Billy watching her silence, her eyes popping open, mouth wailing. Billy shaking his head, this isn't right.

This was after Billy closed red marker-stained fingers around throat, the yellow yarn haired doll, banged its cloth head against wall, against floor. Dangled it by hair over stairs.

This was after days, days of scrawling red splotches, angry red splotches, on white paper.

This was after: "Very naughty, Billy! Very *bad* boy!" And Mr. scrubbing at red marker sprawled three feet high on white hallway wall, squeezing pink water from sponge into soapy bucket, kneeling on stained-red carpet.

This was after marker squeaked against drywall. Angry red splotches. Fist and forearm smeared, stained, shiny wet. Little girl: "I'm telling, Billy!"

This was after days, days of whimpering in sleep, pulling away, sheets and blankets holding too tight. Soft forehead kisses goodnight, "Sleep good, buddy," "This is your new home; you'll like it here." After days, days of watching from a distance little girl play with dolls with baby brother, her crying to Mr. or Mrs., "Billy *hit* me again!" and composed warnings of "Now, Billy, you mustn't hit. Hitting is naughty," and "This is your new home; like it here."

This was after: "Last two families didn't work" and "want to give him another chance."

This was after front door crashing open, splitting to splinters, men in dark clothes with guns shouting, stopping at foot of stairs, leaning over mama, not seeing Billy upstairs hiding under family room table.

This was after Billy pulled at mama's limp arm, "Up, mama, *up!*" Angry voices shouting outside front door. Billy starting to run, tripping over mama's foot, her heel still balanced on second step, picking himself up, running up stairs, sliding under family room table.

This was after Billy standing at top of stairs, ears plugged like cotton balls, a humming sound, watching mama's silence, purple bruising her face, her arms, her body lying on foyer floor, her eyes staring up at ceiling, one leg twisted beneath her, other leg propped up on stairs, heel still balanced on second step.

This was after two days of hiding and peeing and crying and calling out "Daddy?" behind locked bedroom door. No one came.

This was after Billy ran to bedroom, slammed shut door, pushed little lock button not allowed to push, and turned his face into wall, multihued paper border of dump trucks and box trucks and fire trucks mama spread and pressed across room blurring into watercolors, into black. Thunder from hallway: "Open the fucking *door*, you fucking shit!" Billy feeling pounding through forehead, nose flattened against wallpaper; truck-pattern tremoring, an earthquake, heavy fists on door. Until daddy stopped pounding, crying. "I'm sorry. I'm sorry, Billy, I'm fucking sorry." Quiet for a while; then Billy hearing footsteps in hallway. Loud pop like fourth-of-July firecracker. Billy waiting, breathing loud inside head, ears humming. Spinning away from trucks. "Daddy?" Twisting doorknob, snapping unlocked, opening. Daddy in hallway, slouching on floor, wall propping shoulders. Gun Billy not allowed to touch in hand. Hair smeared and stained and shiny wet. Angry red splotches on white wall.

Chalk Dust to Dust

He throttled the shotgun barrel between his fingers, imagining Nadine's throat as he squeezed.

Jaw clenched, Louis decided. He wouldn't give her the satisfaction, not this way.

Clutching to the gun in one hand, a sweating bottle in the other, he instinctively pressed the *Play* button again with his smallest finger. The other four enfolded moist glass, which spread a ring of condensation on an end table.

"Louis, I'm with Scott. I'm done wasting my time on you. On our marriage. Scott and I have been fucking for years, and we're finally able to make this real. I'm taking Anna with me. She's not yours anyway." Nadine paused a moment as if to saturate him with the sting of her last statement. "I'll be there in the morning with papers and to pick up Kitty and some other things. Scott's coming with me."

Staring at nothing, conscious of nothing but the dual comfort of glass and metal, Louis replayed the message.

"Louis, I'm with Scott."

Something racked his spine, caused the beer bottle to swivel noisily against the table. The weight of the gun on his thigh and in his fist suddenly kept him down, and Louis felt he couldn't stand if he tried.

"…fucking for years, and we're finally…"

His gaze dropped to the coffee table in front of him. To the drawer in the middle where he knew a photo album lay, pages closed over wedding photographs, bride and groom clinging to each other, groom and best man coiled inside the blue plume of cigar smoke: Nadine, Louis, and Scott. Nieces, nephews, holiday portraits. Birthday photographs of Annalise Brook, seven years of balloons and cake and candles and pointed party hats.

"She's not yours…"

Seven short years of Halloween costumes, princess dresses and fairy wings, of camping trips and beach vacations, of slumber parties, family holidays, flute recitals. Scott skulking in the backgrounds, a glossy shadow lying in wait. And the damned cat. Hundreds of pictures of that stupid cat whose owner had only enough sense to name "Kitty" after years of post-graduate tuition and alleged late-night library visits, while her husband stayed home with the daughter he loved so much who wasn't his daughter at all.

"Scott's coming with me."

Louis raised the bottle to his lips while, at his ankles, the orange tabby crept around the corner of Louis' recliner and purred against the cuffs of his jeans. The bottle slipped from Louis' fingers and cracked in half against the table, ale foaming and splashing, staining carpet. The cat bolted in the opposite direction, but Louis trapped it against his chair before it could disappear beneath some piece of furniture.

Snatching the cat up by the scruff of the neck, Louis held it at arm's distance from himself, narrowly escaping the hissing, pinpointed teeth and thrashing claws. He moved across the apartment, the ginger feline frantically lashing at him, and heaved open the window with his free hand.

Ducking his head and shoulder through the open window frame, he dangled the frenzied animal over the sidewalk eight stories below. The cat released a high-pitched cry, and, with a front paw, sliced a pair of pink lines across Louis' forearm. Barely aware of the scratch reddening, broadening on his skin, Louis opened his palm and watched the cat somersault through the air.

"Let's see you land on your feet, you fucker."

"You didn't."

"I did."

"You killed her cat." While intending the statement as an accusation, Sharon couldn't suppress the humor from her voice or restrain the corners of her lips from naturally curling upward.

"I couldn't throw myself out the window; that'd just make her happy."

Sharon raised both palms to the sides of her face in mock exasperation and watched the sidewalk as they paced side by side. Louis matched her stride, hands in pockets, head bowed. The twin scabbed stripes on his arm tingled.

"Did you sign the papers?"

"Sharon, I need to ask you." Placing a hand on her arm, Louis turned to face her. "When we were married, did you ever want to, I don't know, take Becky and just…leave?"

"Louis." Sharon's eyes burned sapphire sincerity into his. "I loved you while we were married. You know that. We just…married so young."

Louis began walking again. He stuffed his fists back into his jacket pockets, not necessarily because they were cold, but because he didn't want Sharon to see that his fingers would not unclench. That they shook occasionally, uncontrollably.

Two daughters, he grimaced. *Both being raised by other men.*

"Have dinner with us tonight." Sharon broke into his thoughts. "Spend some time with Becky."

A school bus radiating excited squeals and bellowed name callings crept closer from behind them. Sharon turned at the sound and waved; the driver lifted a hand in reply. As the bus slowed to a stop, opaque shapes behind the windows stood and lurched forward.

"How's she doing?" Louis studied the children's silhouettes, wondering which one was his daughter.

"Are you kidding? Fourth grade is like recess all day long!" Sharon smiled as Becky spilled from the open bus door with other students, laughing and linking arms with another girl.

From across the street, Louis studied his daughter. Four years older than Anna, Rebecca Marie was about the same size as her younger half-sister, petite and wild-eyed like her mother. Sharon's straight auburn hair and freckled cheekbones. Unlike Anna, whose hair and complexion were luminous, personality solemn and secretive like Nadine's, whose entire demeanor inherited none of Louis' qualities or character. But then again, why would it? Neither of Louis' children bore hereditary markers of their paternal genes. Neither wore the dark hair or eyes of Louis' pedigree, nor did they possess any of his aptitudes for science or tears at emotional movies or his aversions to felines and maple syrup. Both girls developed into miniature replicas of their mothers.

"Daddy!" Stepping into the crosswalk, Becky recognized Louis beside her mother and untangled herself from her classmate's arm. She scampered toward him. Releasing his fists from his pockets, Louis scooped his daughter into his arms and boosted her off her feet.

Becky enclosed his neck between her small arms. "I'm so glad you're here," she whispered in his ear.

Squeezing his eyes shut, Louis buried his face in Becky's hair, his fingers slowly prying themselves from fists, fumbling instead for a clutching embrace around his daughter.

*

Along with the days, furniture dashed from Louis' apartment. Appliances, record albums, picture frames, bed sheets, mini blinds. Scott would stand, his back to the door, gaze turned downward, arms crossed, outwardly rejecting any gesture of familiarity with his former college roommate, for whom twice he proudly stood as best man. At one point Louis attempted conversation while standing idly by as DVDs and dishes wandered out of his custody in cardboard boxes, asking sarcastically if Scott enjoyed once again living with all of his shit. "Just like college," Louis sneered as Nadine rounded a corner and told him to go to hell.

One cloudy afternoon, Anna accompanied her mother and Scott to the apartment, her hand locked inside Nadine's, her gaze—so like her biological father's—rubber cemented to the floor. Louis knew this was his chance, his only chance for redemption with his youngest daughter.

As if forecasting his objective, Nadine held tightly to Anna's hand, dragging her from room to emptied room as she rummaged for any forgotten nostalgic or costly knick knack, the small girl chained to her side.

With several small tokens rattling in a large box, Nadine and Anna made their way toward the door where Scott held his post. Louis cornered them. Ignoring Nadine's stone gray admonition, he knelt down before Anna, whose equally gray gaze studied him emotionlessly.

"Anna," was all he could say before the seven-year-old thrust her face toward her mother.

Louis' fingers curled into tight fists at his sides, and warmth drained from his body like a sieve. Anna turned her attention back to Louis but with no intention of responding. Her carbon copy standing three feet taller would handle all further dialogue between the two.

"My lawyer has your number." Nadine pushed past Louis, towing Anna behind her. Scott opened the door and ushered the two out before casting a rapid glance toward Louis on his knees. The door clicked shut behind him, and Louis, kneeling alone in his scantily decorated living room, imagined suddenly pump-loading the shotgun and firing off a magazine between those hailstone eyes.

*

The answering machine was torn so violently from its socket that plaster flew from the wall in all directions. Louis carried the device to his kitchen and slammed it into the trash compactor. Flipping the power switch, he listened to plastic and metal twisting and grinding to confetti. *Let her lawyer get ahold of me now.*

Retrieving his jacket and keys from the recliner, Louis left his apartment to the incessant ringing of the telephone.

Orange and tanned leaves lazily dropped around Louis as he walked the familiar route to Anna's grade school. He hadn't seen her for three weeks, not since she refused to acknowledge him when Nadine packed up the last of their belongings. But he had thought about her. Quite a bit, in fact. Custody papers had arrived several days later, and Louis shredded them and lit fire to the pieces in the kitchen sink.

Dragging his fingers across chain link, Louis observed patches of children spread across the playground. The solitary girl, pale hair pulled back in identical braids, sitting cross-legged on the asphalt, a palette of sidewalk chalk before her, drew Louis' attention. The closest cluster of students was at least sixty yards away playing four-square. The nearest adult was across the playground attending to a scraped elbow.

Interesting, since only a week or two ago, Louis had heard from the pretty brunette newscaster on channel 7 that grade schools in the area were on high-alert due to a pair of kidnappings twenty miles out of the city. Louis felt the impulsive inkling to trudge across the blacktop to the teacher, to threaten calling up the school board for her transparent disregard of lone children sitting complacently within snatching distance from the street.

Blinking hard and shuddering as if suddenly walking through an unexpected cold spot, Louis remembered his walk's intention and focused on the white-blonde braids.

Louis progressed toward her, his fingers bouncing, vibrating over the crisscrossed metal threads. As he moved closer, he faintly heard her humming to herself. Her hands moved swiftly, slid and smeared chalk across multihued rainbows and jack-o-lanterns. Her back to him, only the chain link separating the two, Anna's shoulders hitched slightly when she noticed the shadow cast over her.

She turned only her head toward him, and when she recognized Louis, her shoulders slumped. "Mama doesn't want me to talk to you."

"I know she doesn't." He crouched to her level. "But she's at work."

Anna's light eyes stumbled over his before dropping to the ground. Louis buried his hands in his jacket pockets. *She's been brainwashed*, he realized. She'd turned cold on him. So like her mother.

"I need you to come with me, Anna."

"We're not allowed to leave the playground." Anna returned to her chalk, picking up a stick of green and splotching some grass beneath a purple leering pumpkin.

Louis felt heat rushing into his face. His eyes again located Anna's teacher, now apparently sorting out a fight between two young boys. His hands balled into fists, closed around ice in his pocketed grasp. Fingering the cool metal, Louis leaned forward until his nose nearly poked through a diamond in the fence.

"You don't want mama to get hurt, do you?"

Anna snapped her attention back to Louis as though he had screamed at her. Her eyes widened until two overcast skies stared him in the face. Louis had only seen her this afraid once before when he and Nadine had taken her on the Pirates of the Caribbean ride at Disney Land. Five years old, she had hidden her face against Louis' neck the majority of the ride, occasionally peeking out over his shoulder but only to seize onto his tee shirt again.

"Come with me." Even Louis didn't recognize the voice creeping from his throat. As Anna stood from her chalk colorings, he directed another quick glance toward the teacher.

Anna walked along the fence opposite of Louis, staring at the ground as she moved. She turned once toward her classmates and teacher before exiting the fenced-in yard to Louis, perhaps hoping—unlike Louis—that someone was, in fact, watching.

Louis freed a hand from his pocket and grabbed onto Anna's pink- and green-stained fingers. Together they left the cries of the schoolyard behind them, unseen, as far as Louis was concerned, except for the possibility of a lonely boy parked on a motionless swing.

*

Anna was silent. Louis attempted small talk, but when she would not answer questions about school and Disney movies, he commented on the changing colors of the leaves and remembered aloud a weekend he, Nadine, and Anna had spent camping in the same forest preserve he and Anna walked through now.

"Mama was so scared of bugs and snakes that she left the tent and slept in the car," Louis laughed, clinging absentmindedly to the limp hand in his palm. "Do you remember that? She wanted to leave at three o'clock in the morning when she heard that owl. Remember?"

He vaguely noticed tears coursing down Anna's cheeks, but still she was silent, watching the uneven ground as he led her further into waiting shadows and trees.

"And now mama doesn't want me to be your daddy anymore." Louis flipped the metal in his pocket over and over again between his trembling fingers while his other hand, steady and strong, clutched Anna's. "She wants to take you away from me. She wants Uncle Scott to be your daddy."

Anna sniffled audibly, her cheeks pink, swollen.

"She wants to take you away from me." Louis fought back the tears in his own eyes. "I can't let her do that, Anna. You know why?"

He glanced down at her. He didn't want to admit—even to himself—that the fugitive monster from channel 7 was his inspiration, but the idea did lurk at the base of his skull as he watched—scotch in hand, as the phone rang and rang some more—the brunette report with wide eyes that one of the victims, a ten-year-old from Evansville, had been found, stabbed, off route 57.

"I can't let her do that because, Anna—" He pulled his hand from his pocket, the penknife concealed fully inside his fist. "—no one can take you away from me."

Without warning, Anna flung herself upon Louis, wrapping her arms tightly around his legs. She cried into his jeans, her blonde head bobbing with breathless sobs, her quiet voice muttering once: "Daddy."

Louis' entire body went rigid. With sudden awareness of what he had been about to do, the fog of his rage lifting, clearing, he crumbled to his knees and pulled his daughter tightly to his chest. He was going to kill her. This innocent, sweet baby. He was going to spill her blood over the very spot she had laughed at his ghost stories over a bonfire, where they had roasted marshmallow Peeps left-over from Easter and giggled together over Nadine's hyper-vigilant head jerks toward every twig's snap and draft of wind.

His baby girl.

His joined her tears, and he clutched her firmly, securely to himself. "I'm sorry, baby." His voice slipped through his lips, shaking, forlorn. "I'm so sorry."

Even as he held her, he knew. Nadine would sever any ties he lashed onto their daughter. Losing a second child was inconceivable. Something a father was incapable of allowing. Scattered patches of sunlight warmed his back, tugging him back to the day Anna was born, cradling her miniature form under hot incubation room lights. The porcelain doll he swore he'd never let go of. He knew.

Anna's fingers scratched at his arms and back; her tiny fists beat against his jacket. Her slim body shuddered and convulsed. Still he did not let go.

"I'm sorry. I'm so, so sorry."

After seconds, seconds of holding her to his chest, she stopped stirring. Her arms relaxed and dropped to her sides, her two braids stopped swinging beneath his strong palm, and as Louis loosened his grip on her, her body wilted away from his. Her head sagged away from his chest, her eyes set in that fearful gape she had cast upon him at the playground.

He laid her gently on the ground, and his hands flew up to cover his mouth. Spinning away from her on his knees, he vomited into a deposit of dead leaves. Scotch and bile stung his throat as he threw up and threw up and threw up nothing. A sharp throbbing in his abdomen, unlike anything he had ever felt before, collapsed him to his little girl's side. Wincing, he placed a hand on her forehead, above eyes that gaped in horror at the shedding branches above. With quaking fingers, he pushed her eyelids over the silver irises.

For an hour or more, Louis lay beside Anna, holding her in his arms. Her face, glazed over, innocent. His porcelain doll. Leaves wafted down on them, covering them as if for sleep.

His initial plan entailed weighting her pockets with rocks and stones and easing her downstream in the creek that snaked through the forest preserve. Instead he assisted the branches overhead and carefully arranged leaves and grass around her as if putting her tenderly to bed. He positioned a pile of maple leaves around her head for a pillow and mounded the colorful foliage over her. Lastly, he found a twig twisted into a narrow X and adjusted it, a crooked cross over the knoll of leaves and grass and sticks.

Here a hunter or hiker would come across her and attend to her properly. Louis couldn't stomach the thought of her bloated and bluish body washing up on some litter-strewn canoe launch where some church youth group would shriek and scatter at the sight of her.

Grasping his side, he limped away from Anna, out of the trees, until more and more sun bled through the branches, stung his eyes.

He passed Anna's vacant schoolyard where only the swings swayed in the breeze. He forced his eyes away from the abandoned playground crowded by black asphalt, chain link spider webs, chalk pictures of rainbows and lopsided jack-o-lanterns.

By the time Louis reached his apartment house, sweat rained heavily down his face, and the stabbing pain in his stomach shortened his breath and hunched him over slightly. Reaching into his jacket, he halted abruptly. He pried his keys from the pocket, and, placing them in his palm, fingered each metal carving individually, separating them, studying them. The knife was gone. He shoved fingers into both jacket pockets again, then his jeans pockets, front and back. He pressed his palms against his pocketless chest and returned again to the jacket pockets.

Another realization swept over him like a cold sweat when he noticed that the couple standing outside the apartment building at the intercom was Sharon and her husband. His arm was around her waist. Her hair was flying in all angles about her head, uncharacteristic of Sharon. She was mercilessly hitting the intercom buzzer with her palm.

He turned from the building and rushed to his parking garage. Fumbling through his keys and feeling sick again, he located his car key and ducked into his sedan.

Why the hell was Sharon looking for him? And, more importantly, why was she not alone? Then he remembered. Two of the nine messages indicated by the flashing red light on the late answering machine were from Sharon asking how he was. She was concerned. He would worry about that later; right now, he just wanted to drive, to get away from what he had done, from anyone he knew who might ask questions and expect answers, from those silver staring eyes.

But he couldn't start the car. He couldn't bring himself to twist the key in the ignition.

By the time the sun had sunk beneath the dark horizon and stars poked through the blackness, Louis had crawled—because he could not walk—into a rear corner of the garage. Clasping knees to his chest, lying huddled behind a rusted TA on damp concrete, Louis cried. Buried away from movement outside, Louis only knew that hours were passing and prayed that the owner of the Trans Am would stay in for the night. He drifted into a fitful sleep. A cat somersaulting through the air, white-blond braids flailing, Scott leaning against a doorframe behind Anna blowing out five lit candles, pink sugar melting, dripping off a stale marshmallow Peep, a penknife lost in the leaves glinting in moonlight, the drunken barrel of a shotgun, a smothering embrace, one daughter hopping happily off a school bus, the other's stone gray gaze. Around two o'clock in the morning, Louis woke himself screaming. What he was screaming, even Louis did not know, but it was chilling enough to keep him awake and alert into the morning.

His child was dead. Not by some maniac who collected children from supermarkets and amusement parks. Not by the trained, gloved hands of a man who lured the young and naïve to his side, to their deaths. But by these hands that trembled and tremored and fastened into fists before Louis' eyes.

Plan A had to be resurrected.

Squinting early morning sun from his eyes, Louis vaguely perceived the waiting figures at the mouth of the parking garage. When the trio of officers drew their 9mms, Louis had tears in his eyes, not because he felt caught, trapped—both of which were undeniably true—but because this was a delay of his plan. When they cocked the hammers, Louis knew.

They found her.

He offered his empty palms without a word and allowed one of the officers to cuff his hands behind his back. The man's words fired syllabic puffs of air at the back of Louis' neck, but the sounds themselves never reached Louis' ears. Voluntarily deaf, he surmised, and allowed his captor to heave him into the back seat of a squad car. Louis rested his face against the cool glass for the entirety of the ride to the police station two blocks from his apartment building where his shotgun waited friendless, eight floors up, abandoned in his bedroom closet.

"Here's the situation." A large plain-clothes officer, a detective perhaps, towered over Louis who sat at a table in a room occupied by only that table, four chairs, and a two-way mirror across one wall. "Early this morning, a young girl's body was found. She's been identified as your daughter."

Louis cradled his head in his hands, focusing on the spiderweb-like cracks etched into the tabletop under his elbows. Breath erupted from his lungs in spasms; he felt as though he might, at any moment, choke to death on his own air.

"Your ex-wife is here, Mr. Macklin," the man said, shifting his eyes fleetingly to the mirror at Louis' left. "She's been trying to get a hold of you. Hasn't been able to. For weeks. And now this, your daughter—"

"I'm sorry." Louis' voice, barely audible, left a buzz in the air that he could feel on his skin.

"Are you confessing, Mr. Macklin?" The man leaned over Louis, his heavy fist propping his weight up on the table. "Are you confessing to the murder of your daughter?"

"I'm sorry," Louis muttered. "I just couldn't...without her..."

A soul-piercing wail of utter despair rang through the room, snapping Louis' face out of his hands. He recognized the voice, but he didn't expect to hear it here, not hers. A door beside the mirror flew open, and Sharon plunged through the frame, still screaming.

"Sharon?" Louis rose to his feet. The detective hurled a strong arm across Louis' chest to keep him from taking a step toward Sharon. Two uniformed officers hurried after Sharon, each grabbing hold of an elbow.

"Why *Becky*, Louis?!" Sharon's voice swelled and dipped with a bestial timbre. It was strange and frightening in Louis' ears. "Why Becky? She's *yours*! How could you do this to Becky?!"

"No, Sharon, I would never—!" Pitching forward into the man's muscled forearm, the sharp pain in Louis' abdomen reawakened and nearly sank him to the carpet.

Sharon's knees buckled, and the two officers caught her before she plummeted to the floor. With Sharon's red-brown hair falling in tangles over her face, her features hidden from view, Louis could only listen as her wailing disintegrated into gut-wrenching moans, inhuman and haunted.

"Where's your knife, shithead?" Louis spun back around to face the detective. He searched the man's face for clarity, for any semblance of an explanation. "Where is the murder weapon?"

"Wha—What?" The throb in his side rising to a peak, Louis doubled over in pain.

"Where is your knife, you son of a bitch?" The man held Louis in a semi-standing position, disallowing him to collapse back into his chair. "The one you used to stab and murder your daughter, Rebecca?"

"No, I—I didn't...I..."

The room swelled again with Sharon's cries of anguish, Louis left crutched and agonized over a policeman's arm, shifting his glance between the man and Sharon, hopelessly willing one of them to explain to him what in God's name had happened.

What Louis wasn't yet aware of was that down the hall, Nadine sat rigid with another detective, wringing and twisting a damp tissue between her fingers, her stony eyes wide and red-rimmed, the search for her daughter, the detective regretted to inform her, still at nothing, though they had managed to track down her ex-husband and would be questioning him in minutes; that blocks away, a pair of police officers were pulling a loaded shotgun from Louis' bedroom closet while others pried open drawers and cabinets, rifled through files and linens and photo albums; that just miles away, a Boy Scout troop entered the local forest preserve, their mission to clean up litter, trash leftover at campsites and boat launches, to wander around in pairs with shiny garbage bags, to comb carefully through the trees and the leaves.

Schatten

The two scurry along a long corridor, cower close to the walls, quiet like mice, vigilant for shadows on thresholds and big figures rounding corners. The girl clutches to her brother's sleeve. In the boy's arms, a baby in a blanket, eyes closed and cheeks pink. They shouldn't be here, they know. Above all, they know, as they've been warned, they mustn't be seen.

Voices.

Anna clings to Herman's arm, and they dart into a dark companionway, a ladder leading further down below deck. Herman tightens his grasp on the unmoving infant in his arms and motions for Anna to keep quiet. The weight in his arms presses on him, and he wants to move. The voices grow louder, closer; the dialect is High German, and the two don't understand. Anna's eyes fix on Herman's. The two barely breathe.

A group of grown-ups shuffles past their hiding place, long dresses rustling, shoes clicking and clomping, voices trailing away. Undiscovered, the pair expels a shared exhale. Cautiously, Herman peers around the wall, watches the shadows veer away. He leads Anna back out into the passageway, and they dash toward clanging dishes and rushing water. Earlier this morning, they had overheard Mutti and Oma speaking about work in the galley.

The sounds lead them to the loud gaping space where harried women hunch over sinks and troughs, swipe at dripping dishes with damp, dirty cloths, where steam curls up around their red and raw faces. Herman bites his lip and scours the room with jumpy eyes; Anna spots their mother first.

Mutti!

All women turn toward the cry. Children's voices sound the same. Necks crane, pivot around other women and kitchen equipment. Children's clothing looks the same. Eyes squint, strain through dim lighting toward the faces, search out distinguishing features—hue of hair, contour of cheek. Children were not allowed in the galley, were not allowed anywhere other than the space below deck for sleeping and reading and daily lessons for songs and nursery rhymes, which should be taking place as the two appear, blanket-wrapped infant clutched in the boy's arms.

Mutti!

Bertha Schulz wrings her hands, numb and red from scalding water, in her apron. Face flushed, hair twisted and tangled and fallen in places from a loose bun at the back of her head. The stout woman alongside her takes soundless helm at the sink as Bertha steps toward her children. Other women rally back into routine as maternal claim falls away. All chatter, clanging, splashing resume.

Herman? Anna?

Mutti, das Baby ist heiss.

Lifting one palm, pulse to forehead, Bertha moves quickly, skirt hem trailing through grease and soapy drainage, fingers still busy in apron, curling, clenching, extending, attempting to regain feeling.

Herman holds the baby, wrapped in one of three blankets the family of six shared, outstretched toward his approaching mother. Anna stands silently beside him, several inches shorter, eyes blue and wide.

Collecting the infant in her arms, Bertha presses her wrist to the child's face. The skin tingles but without temperature, her own skin anesthetized by dishwater. She raises the child to her cheek, warmth radiating from within the thin fabric.

A woman working nearby sets silverware onto the countertop and paces over, placing a hand each on Herman's and Anna's shoulders. Anna gazes up at the stranger and explains:

Without pause the woman reaches over to Bertha, touching the baby's cheeks, forehead, neck, chest, cheeks again. She finds Bertha's eyes, nods.

Bertha urges the children from the galley, through a long hallway, past a large and loud laundry room. For nine hours a day, women take turns in groups to wash clothes and dishes, to cook and bake, to take care of children, to read to them, to teach them. They clean, oil, paint, and repair. Some are nurses, tending to the sick. And so many are sick. Some also work as maids for the upstairs passengers. The men work on deck, on the engines, cleaning and oiling and mending what is broken. Every other day, women and their children surface for fresh air, to look into the waves and sky, to point in the supposed direction of their unseen new home, to hold hands and spin in circles, to shadow the deck from sunlight. For one hour. The rest of the days and nights are spent below, crowded but comfortable enough, sitting and sleeping on the floor.

On this, day seventeen of a journey from Germany to America, Wilhelm Schulz stoops over one of the ship's rails, hammer in hand, nails clamped between teeth, taste of steel on his lips and tongue, sunsweat darkening his shirtback. He enjoys the work. Even though it leaves his back and joints aching, he trusts his efforts will pay out in the end. The harder the challenge, the sweeter the reward. Seek and ye shall find, knock and it shall be opened, ask and it shall be given unto you.

America is not Anklam.

Behind him is old Germany. A fruitful but ended enlistment to the Kaiser and his army. A past of manual labor and starvation. A child buried in hard Anklam soil. His brother will be wounded in the upcoming war, never to join him in the States. His mother and sister-in-law will watch each other wither and expire, clawing at their stomachs in hunger. He knows none of this. Only looks ahead.

Ahead is change. Opportunity for his three children, his wife, his wife's mother. Education. Satisfied sweat on his back. Paycheck in hand. The old has passed away; behold, the new has come. By God, he would provide for his family.

A slap to his shoulder and a nod from his partner forces his attention away from his repairs. Hastening toward him is his wife, Bertha, white-blonde hair flying, apron sodden and stained, a bunched blanket seized in her arms. His mother-in-law stands several yards back with four-year-old Herman and two-year-old

Anna before her. Wilhelm grimaces as he stretches his spine to a vertical angle. Before he can speak, his wife's eyes, glazed and pained, wild, are on his. Something plummets in his gut, the hammer coming down.

Das Baby ist kalt.

**

The moment of release. Fingertip mutiny. Skin leaving skin. Instantaneous panic. Horror. Hysteria. Excruciating urge once without grasp to snatch flesh back again, clutched to chest, breath unrequired for love, for solace, for eternal embrace. Bitter wind scales the throat. Arms stretch forth, empty palms open heavenward as if awaiting deliverance.

A baby dropped.

A quiet splash.

Wilhelm stands close, his hands ballasts of composure on her shoulders, his breath drafting prayers against her ear. Bertha gazes into the waves while the pale form submerges, dims and extinguishes, becomes one with black, black water. She sinks with it. Even her arms, stretched before her, seem to float upward under new weightlessness, buoyant on an unseen current.

Still Wilhelm's grip anchors her, his litany ascending to the stars while she and her child plunge ever lower into depths untouched but by shadow.

How many ships? How many children? How many babies born, mourned, and buried at sea? Corpses cradled in sheaths of ocean algae. A sunless nursery of infant skeletons at the bottom. Bertha yearns for nothing but to dive down and scour the Atlantic's floor, gathering bones.

Twelve children scattered into the sea since leaving port. Half the voyage remained.

Wilhelm sings now, his voice low, his eyes shut.

Wer nur den lieben Gott lässt walten

Und hoffet auf ihn allezeit

Peering down into liquid shadows, Bertha's eyes focus on a shape emerging, materializing just below the swell. Her arms slowly droop until palms alight on the ship's thin rail. The vision bobs to the surface. A bone. Gaunt and diminutive like a chicken bone, but Bertha knows what it is.

Den wird er wunderlich erhalten

In allem Kreuz und Traurigkeit.

Her husband's voice, soft and singing sweetly to his great and good God, fades away, background noise like the waves slapping the sides of the ship. One by one, Bertha sees, bones—little ones—bubble and poke to the surface. Tiny skulls, orange-sized, with yawning eye sockets, clavicles, femurs, fingers, bobbing and floating, side by side, crowding the hull of the ship. Bertha imagines them fragile as matchsticks. Kindling. To breathe upon one might split it cracking in half. The sea ensconced with them. The moon shines on them, reflecting its white light. So littered with bones is the water that Bertha imagines the passengers could climb overboard and walk across, snapping and splintering, all the way to the States.

More. Bertha knows; more will die. She will bury more children.

**

At five years old, Bertha stood, knife in hand, over a chopping block. Her mother pivoted between bacon spitting over a wood fire and various boiling pots. Bertha's young sister Minnie explored the room, overseeing the luncheon preparations, humming to herself, explaining to her doll what was a potato, what was a storm cloud, what was a knapweed embroidered on a tablecloth. Outside, their father walked behind two horses tethered to a plow, hoping to turn the dirt before the gathering storm pelted the fields with early spring rain.

Bertha brushed absently at her eyes with her forearm, onion tears dampening her cheeks.

Distant thunder grumbled and coughed, vibrated the floors. Several glass candle lamps placed strategically around the kitchen cast dim dancing shadows on the walls and ceiling.

Minnie mumbled to herself, her voice airy and melodic

Das Baby ist kalt!

and she lovingly laid one of their father's handkerchiefs over her little doll's stiff body.

A gust of warm air burst through the open kitchen door, flickering candle flames and momentarily swirling the girls' hair up around their faces. Bertha shivered as a flash of lightning shocked the room with false daylight. Glancing around to make sure none of the candles needed relighting, her gaze stopped on her mother who stood stiff and straight. Her mother's eyes, suddenly distant, widened with inexplicable knowledge, with impossible vision, as though someone mysterious and invisible had whispered something dreadful into her ear. A stoneware pitcher slipped from her fingers, and she made no attempt to catch it before it crashed heavily onto the floor.

Minnie, who had been cooing unintelligibly to her doll, plopped to the floor as well, wailing, startled by the noise. Bertha dismissed her chopping block and dropped to her sister's side to hush and comfort the toddler.

Rain started to fall in loud exhales from the sky.

Sister embraced, Bertha watched her mother stand frozen, earthenware shards ignored at her feet. She had never seen her mother like this before. Her head began moving gently side to side, then faster. Whatever she was hearing, she was denying.

Nein, her mother muttered without breath. Her fingers coiled into fists at her sides, gathering layers of skirts. Trance broken, she rushed through the room and out into the rain.

Nein

Bertha pulled Minnie to her feet, and, hands chained together, they ran after their mother, into the storm. Rain hit them like stones.

...nein nein nein...

Fat, chilled drops of rain drenched the girls just yards from the house. The ground was quickly becoming mud that splashed and spattered their long dresses. Minnie stumbled; Bertha bent to pick her up, plant her on a hip the way her mother so often did, but she wasn't strong enough, hadn't hip enough. She nearly sprawled into the muck herself. Instead she dabbed at her sister's blackened elbow and knees with her apron and coaxed the little one on.

Overhead, dark clouds strobed and groaned, simultaneous lightning and thunder. Bolts of electricity shredded the sky. Cracks and booms shook the earth. Bertha struggled to catch up with her mother, but the gap only widened with Minnie's short stride.

Ahead, their mother stopped fast, her shoes sliding a bit over wet grass, her back to her daughters; her fingers flew up to her hair and tore at soaked strands.

A bitter moan, low and haunted, rose into the air, snagged Bertha's breath. Even Minnie spun her face into her older sister's side, away from the sound. Another scream, this one inhuman, a horse's terrorcry. Purple branches of lightening slashed across heaven, bolded the two horses wild. Up they reared and ran. An explosion of noise.

Thunderstampede.

A mother on her knees.

A father trampled beneath panicked hooves.

**

Below deck Wilhelm balances Anna and Herman each on a knee, points, waves, laughs at the Statue of Liberty through the small open porthole. Their happy voices pitch and bounce with the surf that sprays and sighs against the body of the ship, thick salt in the air, stinging the lips, tasted on the tongue. Bertha sits away, her back to the wall, staring into her lap. Her empty arms slack at her sides. Her mother watches her in silence.

Plots

Clara was the second woman Jack buried.

Grown grandchildren each take an elbow and usher the old man slowly forward, the suction of sodden earth tugging at their shoes. The long stem of his cane punctures the ground at regular intervals, belches free after every second shuffle-step.

Amethyst clouds hover low, close overhead. No rain yet, but the air leaves a chilled dampness on the skin that no amount of writhing can dispel.

And Jack does writhe. His collar and sleeves stick to his skin. He focuses on the gloved hands of the pallbearers to divert attention from his discomfort; none seems to strain under the varnished box, Clara barely eighty pounds laid to rest. In the distance skulk the North Woods or, as his father's generation called them, the *Na'wds*. Though they've been a permanent fixture of Jack's upbringing, he still suppresses a shudder and lowers his gaze. Half-afraid, perhaps expecting to encounter the wraith's shape shadowed against the treeline.

> *Them trees'll swallow a man whole*
>
> *Never t'spit 'm back out again.*
>
> *Denser'n the caverns a' hell.*

Jack feels the twin grasp on his arms tighten as the men ahead slow to a stop and carefully set the casket on a makeshift stand before his wife's gravestone.

Clara Tanner

Beloved wife of fifty-seven years.

Adored mother, grandmother.

Sister in Christ.

His own name to the right, awaiting deposit.

A man from the mortuary passes around dark roses from a memorial wreath that had been propped on an easel during the visitation until each relative holds one. At his side, Jack's granddaughter lifts hers to her nose.

A fresh surge of grief sweeps over him, snags breath mid-inhale. A clouded image of twenty-year-old Clara creeps to existence from his memory and settles in his throat. Fifty-seven precious years of marriage, and the early stretch was what Jack couldn't help but dwell on since Clara died four days before. Spring into summer into fall, a bitter wind stalked their brief honeymoon, winter's pall a shapeshifter of weight loss and sunken eyes. A newlywed couple spat prematurely into the throes of decrepitude. As the cancer burrowed itself deeper into her abdomen, digging its barbed foothold in for longevity, Jack glimpsed the woman he had feared he might never see in actuality, an aged version of the kid he married. A woman so broken, so weak, so depleted that she couldn't smooth her own hair with a comb. A face so drawn, so grayed with malady she had begged him to drape all the mirrors in the house with tablecloths and bedsheets, for even as he carried her past, the sight of her own appearance was too upsetting, too haunting, too scary.

And this cloudy reminiscence of his cherished, damaged bride inextricably invoked another image, another face, another name, a harlot's name.

"I'll suck you off for a drink."

Candy.

Even now, so many years, a lifetime, later, the name sours his stomach. That name, a rancid mass that throbs and spreads, scratches its way up his throat to where he can almost taste it on his tongue. It pulls his gaze toward the branches shedding their colors in the distance.

Blately's boy gone huntin'

never come home.

While her cohorts birthed babies and traded recipes for corned beef, Clara spun the revolving door between a hospital in Connecticut and a suitcase in her own bedroom. During chemotherapy's experimental stages, Jack staved off fate's jinx by resisting the habitual urge to purchase round trip train tickets. He dutifully hopped the railway south every time the phone call from her doctor suggested another weekend's recovery in her own home. The few nights a month Clara spent with him, she whimpered like a frightened child in her sleep, and he pressed his lips to her face until she calmed, whispering words even he didn't hear.

And his bed had grown cold.

"You poor, poor man." Painted fingernails stroking.

Though he fought the craving to reduce himself to the status of other broken men who sipped on scotch in public and staggered home on fumes at dawn, temptation surpassed his noble intentions. It wore mascara, a short skirt, and stockings, flesh-colored. He was lonely. He was thirsty. And a serpentine grin across the room recognized the type.

Candy was a drifter, trash blown in from New York City. Her breath hot on his throat, a hint of clove rousing his nostrils.

He hadn't believed his wife would survive the cancer years. His greatest mistake had been dwindled hope. A young bride half-buried in his mind. A breathing, pulsing, dark-eyed stranger with a beckoning finger and a snow-white smile.

A gray drizzle spits onto the bowed heads of the mourners. A memory silhouetted beneath the trees in Jack's thoughts. Dark eyes open, unblinking as the first flakes fell from a March nightsky. Arthritic fingers strangle a burgundy rose.

Ol' Patty Thorland took his rifle 'n shot hisself back there

'n wa'n't found 'til grouse season start up again

The sweet scent of the perfumed bloom rises to his nostrils, and he bites back the urge to gag, for underneath the flower smell is another, one putrid and bitter, of things rotting.

"Jackson?" Clara's voice wafted through the hallway from the bedroom, feeble and concerned. "Jackson?!"

"S'all right. I'll be right in."

Jack heard his voice betray his words. It wouldn't be all right. Not with this wench darkening the threshold. Taking a decisive step forward, he blocked the intruder's path into the house. He lowered his tone to a growl. "Get on outta here."

"Has poor Clara come home at last?" Her voice was a child's. High-pitched and sing-song deliberate. Playful ignorance widened Candy's mascara-blackened eyes.

"I told you…" Jack inched closer and bent his face toward her. "…to get outta here."

Candy tipped her head to one side in mock perplexity. Her dark eyes danced between Jack's and the hallway over his shoulder, eyeing the empty space the way a snake might fix its gaze on an injured bird. The sun was setting behind her, Jack could see, dipping slowly beyond the peak of the Finlays' roof across the street. Her shadow spilled into his house, an uninvited yet undeterred presence. One corner of her mouth hitched into a wicked smirk. "I came here to tell you something. Something important."

"Get. Out. A'here." His voice was a grumble of far-off thunder.

"Jackson Tanner, who's that at the door?" Clara called. Jack detected panic singeing the syllables of his wife's muffled plea, curling the edges. He pictured her struggling, skeletal against the sheets, summoning the strength to swing her legs over the side of the bed.

"Something you should know." Candy tenderly cradled her hands against her stomach, her smirk widening, slithering across her lips.

It was her mouth that finally set him off. That mouth that contorted and sneered and propositioned and promised things, vile things, things that now swept on pin-prick little feet up and down Jack's arms and spine, that brought bile burning, boiling up into his throat. Jack seized Candy's face between both of his hands, far too roughly to be construed as romantic, even by her. Her eyes enlarged again, this time in alarm. With a violent jerk, he brought her face close to his, so their foreheads nearly touched, so she winced into his eyes.

"You will not come here again."

He heaved her from himself. She stumbled backwards across the porch, heeled shoes tangling in each other, arms pin-wheeling. Jack shut the door before she regained her balance and retreated through the hallway, avoiding the windows as he stalked past.

Clara's tired anxiety met his gaze as she lay tense and coiled in blankets.

"A telegram f'the Finlays across the street," he told her. "Wrong house."

He dropped to her side and palmed her forehead as if feeling for a fever, kissed her chilled skin.

She drifted into a fitful sleep, and every time one of her full-bodied shudders racked her thin frame, he squeezed her tightly to himself. Clara would never know, Jack told himself. She would never know about his lonely nights, the barstool propositions, Candy, his weak infidelity. He loved his wife, loved her more than his own life, and by God he wasn't about to let some jezebel creep in like a second cancer to stake any claims. This disease he could fight.

With the sun, Jack's thoughts sank down between the twisted black branches of the North Woods. He remembered prying clots of dirt from his cleats, sitting on his mitt on dust on third base, waiting, waiting for Jimmy Blately to show up to play shortstop. He remembered his father and Ol' Man Miller and Ronnie Finlay marching in a silent line side by side toward the treeline, hands in pockets, heads low, while his mother tried without success to calm Mrs. Thorland who wept and flapped a piece of torn paper through the air. He remembered his own feet pounding, leaves and twigs and bristles pulling at his hair, at his letterman jacket, at his blue jeans, catching in his shoelaces, the black boy casting sweaty, frightened glances over his shoulder at the group advancing, laughing.

Candy never made the headlines. And Jack never regretted what he had to do. After Clara had fought so hard, come back home to stay, Jack could not permit anything to collapse their plans for a life and family together. He never regretted what he had to do.

And it was nothing like these sadistic fucks today. Soulless fiends who stopped blameless breath. Who stuffed children into sleeping bags and suitcases. Who came after whole families, classrooms of kids, simply because they were shoved around too many times, seen and treated as the weaklings they were. They acted, not because they had to, but because they felt like it, because they could. Jack wasn't one of them. He was a man, a family man. He'd only done what he had to do.

After the cancer years, after the dirty end of winter melted away into a hopeful spring, after the mirrors shed their tablecloths and bedsheets, Clara gave birth to a son, a stillborn daughter, and another son. Before the nurses took the dead child away, they swaddled her in a small blanket and placed her in Jack's arms. "You, sweet girl," he murmured to the child as if she was only sleeping, "you're the one I didn't deserve to have." And he planted a soft kiss on her pale blue forehead before the women carried her away.

The nightmares started shortly after his daughter's birth and death. He'd awaken sweating, sticking to the sheets, clutching his pillow between shaking fists. He'd climb quietly out of bed, careful not to wake Clara, and tiptoe to his son's room. By the time their second son was born, Jack followed a nightly routine; he'd awaken startled and soaked in sweat, check on the boys, feed or change one of them when necessary, then pace the windows that faced north, peering with a keen vigilance into the night. In the dark, the distant treeline was invisible, shadows strangling shadows, but Jack felt sure he would detect the slightest deviation, the pale emergence of flesh against black, the faint aroma of decay unearthed and unbound, the sudden snap of a twig. Yes, even from this great distance, windowpane to treeline, Jack was confident his senses, practiced and astute, would perceive the breach between waking nightmares and the reality in which his family slept warm and complacent in their beds. So he paced. A nocturnal sentry keeping watch.

In daylight, Jack knew better. In daylight, he knew she was probably never found.

First of all, you had to know where to look.

"If a man want his business his own, he get away with it in them nor'easter' backwoods." Quoting his father that night in March, long before the boys were born, long before the nurses carried the blue baby away, this is what Jack told her as he led her by the hand into the trees. She gushed something passionate and clung tighter to his fist.

Like them high school kids chased that colored boy

back in there and wouldn'ta got caught 'cept

that one a their mothers sent in his lil' sister to call f'dinner,

went hollerin' home to her daddy…

Secondly, someone needs to look.

No one ever came for her—except for that narrow-eyed whore sister of hers. Pounding on every door and thrusting the black and white glossy into family men's faces, their wives bristling at their elbows. Her fingernails painted a chipped and bloody purple.

More than likely, she had never been found, or, if she had been, she had lain unnamed and unclaimed on a cold, metallic slab awaiting identification before turning to ash and stashed in a plastic urn on some mortuary's basement storage shelf. Place-card reading Jane Doe or Heap of Bones or Sorry Whore. Perhaps, Jack thinks, she waits there still.

Or perhaps, she is still where he planted her that night in March so many years ago, securely buried under forty inches of slack dirt and forty more of fresh morning-after snow. Black-smudged eyes open and unblinking. The first lazy flakes just beginning to fall.

*

Jack slapped the boy across the face. Then he yanked the other one from behind his brother and slapped him too. A fistful of fragmented twigs dropped to the grass from the little one's grasp. "What'd I tell you boys? You stay outta them woods! Hear me? Stay the hell outta there!"

"But we heard her in there, Pop." The little one rubbed his cheek, tears pooling his eyes. "We heard her."

Jack turned toward his older son, crouched down to stare him in the eyes. "What'd you hear back in them trees, boy?"

Behind Jack, a door banged open and shut, and Clara called out from the porch, "Jackson? Jackson, is everything all right?"

The little one tore away toward his mother, crying and still clinging to his flushed cheek. Jack knew without looking that Clara would envelope the stricken boy into her adoring embrace, wrap her protective wings around his small trembling shape, coo gentle words of comfort and care, the moment he met her fingertips, and Jack treasured her for it.

His older son met his gaze, a pink flower blooming bravely on his own cheek.

"Nothin', Pop. We didn't hear nothin'."

*

In the confession box nine months before Clara's funeral, Jack acknowledged for the first time his recurring dream.

Always comin' outta them woods

Shadows partin' like some goddamn stage curtains

Always holdin' somp'n in her a'ms

Her fingernails black 'n torn like she clawed her way out

Always holdin' somp'n in her a'ms.

Soft fingers squeeze Jack's elbow. "Grandpa?"

Peering into the distance, Jack had been scowling into branched shadows. At the gentle coaxing of his granddaughter's fingers, his grasp relaxes around a fistful of petals which fall to the grass without so much as a whisper.

Undertow

You steady your hand around the utility knife and slice an even line, shoulders hitched slightly against the zipping tear of the packing tape. You're careful not to cut too deep, cognizant of the shallow contents.

Folding back flaps, you move slowly, breath held back in your throat, eyelids pinched almost shut, fighting to stay closed. Dread is a slowly melting mass of ice in your stomach. And this is only the first box. Christmas morning for the damned.

But it must be done.

You force your eyes open and gulp in the stale aroma of stored-away things, objects atticked and locked in cardboard shadows for eleven years, belongings appearing only in fading photographs and stubborn nightmares.

Spread across the top is a grayed-purple blanket, plush and stitched with the oversized outline of a yellow thread giraffe, the curve of its spine frayed and poking gold hairs in odd directions, the casualty of a dryer incident thirteen years prior.

You lift the fabric gently, fingertips almost remembering the soft grain. Before realizing it, you pull the blanket to your nose and inhale the must-covered cloth, nostrils detecting a muted but very real trace of smoke.

Even now, over a decade and two-hundred-and-some miles away, you still feel that pull, that magnetic tug that has nothing to do with want. You like to think that if you could erase those years, if you could imprint something different over that stretch of time the way you used to tape over an old radio song on a cassette, you would.

You selfish monster. You murderous bitch.

You started running the day after the funeral, a few days after the fire. No one actually blamed you for it, not out loud. No one said, "This is your fault." But people have a way of prickling at the back of your neck when they're not looking at you. Of buzzing in your ear when no one utters a word. Of leaving your skin chilled and sticky when they let your change drop a few inches into your palm.

You tell yourself it would have been better never to have lived those six years than to look back on them and remember. You tell yourself to pretend he never existed, that he never celebrated those few birthdays. And these are the thoughts that leave your head feeling detached from your body, hovering, floating up and up like a child's balloon.

Each day after felt more mountainous. Prying yourself up and out, clawing and climbing to slip back down a few feet to claw and climb back to where you'd already been. Peaking the day finally at filling out the easy half of the insurance form or bringing the paper in from the driveway or addressing the envelope or shaving your legs. Then careening face first back over the other side. A refrigerator magnet. A single sock caught at the bottom of the washer. A thumbprint faint and ornate on a window pane. Remnants.

The phone calls. The scripted cards. The dying flowers no one thought to throw away. The trinkets and toys left on the porch. Flickering candle jars and clay crafted stepping stones with scriptures engraved and pastel wildlife with their too-wide eyes and crying smiles.

The Sunday School class pasted together a poem, a collage they called it, of crayoned memories and Bible stories and pictures from the summer picnic of face paint and snow cones.

Your daughter was only two at the time, and short stretching fingers scraped and scratched at items you now considered sacred. Everything was boxed up. Stacked and stashed beneath basement stairs until you left. And each time you've moved, the taped-shut boxes have come with you, always to be shoved into some attic or crawlspace or basement closet, but never opened. Tangible baggage.

The blanket you smooth over your lap. The stuffed animals and Matchbox cars and brontosaurus figurines you place with delicate contemplation into your suitcase. It all has to fit.

And it's time to leave. Because if you don't leave again, you'll lose your goddamned mind. And not in that peaceably numbed, no grasp on reality, rocking back and forth, clutching onto children's stuffed bears, grinning at nothing into the distance sense of losing your mind.

You don't deserve the peace, you sadistic bitch.

No, staying in this town would result in the variety of losing your mind where every window you passed on every drive, where every window you passed on every walk over cracked sidewalks would frame his glowing face. Where every box fan and running faucet and heat register and droning lawn mower would whine his cry. Where every neighbor taking out the trash on Tuesdays, every restaurant server jotting down your meager, low-cal lunch order, every supermarket cashier demanding to see your 40-something-year-old birthdate on your ID as she slides bottles, bottles of Merlot over the conveyor, every janitor sloshing a mop as you lock up the building after work at night would one by one start to recognize

You're the one. You're the heartless murderer.

Your husband was the first to leave. He packed your little girl and enough clothes to last a month and drove away. Though it took more time before your attempted escape, you started running long before he did.

Mornings spent crouched at the bottom of a concrete staircase, caressing cardboard surfaces. Even neighbors who peered through gaps in drapes couldn't tell whether anyone was in the house. Even the men working upstairs who tarped the roof and replaced the walls in the afternoons couldn't say for sure whether you were home. They let themselves in and out with a duplicate of your key and scaled the stairs to the second story in silence. One neighbor, a bleeding heart with two small children of her own took your daughter in during the days because she said she couldn't stand to hear the child whimpering through the screens.

Three tiny tee shirts you roll and pinch into a gap between toys in your luggage. His favorites. Stained and paled from wear.

Your daughter's face began to change, to resemble another face, a murdered boy's face, her brother's face, and for that, you withdrew from her, left her to fuss in her crib, often hungry, often in a wet diaper, while you cowered with cardboard boxes.

I could hear the poor child from my backyard. The poor thing. Where was her mother? Where the hell was her mother?

A woman from the PTA still forwards town newsletters: reminders that the annual Settlers' Celebration is quick approaching; the library erected a new wing; the council members are debating over a new jogging path alongside the pond; reminders that the kindergarten class had traded training wheels for drivers' licenses; they were working first jobs serving fast food and stocking store shelves; they were planning a nautical-themed senior prom: *A Night to Remember.*

Heat flushes your face as you fasten the canvas lid over so many resurrected memories. Souvenirs from a life that fought so hard to be submerged, but kept poking and bobbing to the surface. Heavier than it looks, the suitcase bounces the car on its tires when it tumbles into the back seat. Wrapping the lavender blanket around your shoulders like a shroud, you creep out of the garage, glancing both ways as if for traffic, but really just to take a last look at the latest neighborhood. Overhead the sky is sullen, glowering and gray, the sun's set undetected beneath smoky clouds. The air feels impossible to breathe.

The flames that snarled and growled that night, lashing at starless nightsky. A small boy's choked cries behind a steadfast door. Time, clean air enough to save only one. A sleeping girl curled in the crook of quaking arms. Waiting on the front lawn longing, looking up. The vacant upstairs window that echoed strobing light.

Where the hell was his mother?

Tightening his small blanket around your neck and shoulders against the heavy air, you turn back to the car, climb inside, twist the key in the ignition. Time to run again. Your suitcase a shadowed bulk in the back seat reflected in the rearview. You crank the windows down, inhale deeply the exhaust, shut your eyes.

The garage door groans, shuts, keeps the outside light from getting in, the smoke from getting out.

Like Father

It's in that instant, the sudden fear in her eyes, the whites widening as he draws his arm back, fingers bending into a swift fist, poised for the punch, that he almost remembers the voices in the hall, one deep as hell, spitting, the other one shrill and pleading. The words escape him, his past. An explosion of light, of sound, a lamp, a bulb shattering against the wall, like a skull, the belt, the fist, the boot to the soft giving flesh of the gut, a handful of his mother's hair. And now, inside the abrupt surprise in her eyes as he pulls back his fist, he almost remembers a mother and her boy cowering in a corner in the big man's shadow, the devil himself, baby teeth rattling, cupping the spilling blood in hands, afraid of a stain on a clean pressed shirt. And now, what kind of man would he be to take her lip, to split it, to *punch her lights out*, feed her a *knuckle sandwich*, and he almost remembers the crack, the splinter of bone, a skull, rebounding off the wall, the plaster branching into spiderwebs, hair tearing from a scalp, and they were just baby teeth, blood dripping into cupped hands, the monster of a man looming, looking down on her, on her boy. The fear inside him, the boy, now, the fire. And now, in that moment as she recoils before the blow, eyes wide, dread inside, he can't quite remember because, like bruises, some things fade, even blunt trauma forgotten.

(Re)Claiming Sanctuary

As if I could break into fucking smaller pieces.

3B catches my eye briefly before changing course; she turns on her heel and ducks back down into the stairwell. Perhaps she's forgotten something in her apartment, needs to retrieve it before heading out. Of course, her apartment is upstairs, not down.

Eyes averted, shoe analysts, all of them. I've made it a habit of examining forehead creases myself. The notch that won't smooth itself from between the eyebrows. The glint of nonsweat begging to break free but disallowed, urged to hold off until safely up the next flight of stairs.

"…don't know how to say…"

"…we're just…"

"… w e ' r e   s o …"

One of my neighbors picks up my mail. Leaves it in a wicker basket by my door. It's not even my basket. I want to think it's just someone offering a small favor. A subtle gesture suggesting sympathy.

More often, however, I'm afraid they just don't want to run into me in the lobby.

But apparently that's being paranoid.

*

My therapist wants to know what I'm feeling.

weighed down

so weighed down

"You feel 'way down?' Or 'weigh-*duh* down?'"

Okay fine, I feel

way-down-weighed-down. I am so

tired of being . . . of just

b e i n g

"So, what do you want to be?"

And I hang myself from my father's basement rafters.

*

Life as an outpatient is liberating. Dropped by cab at the visitor's entrance, I am anyone. I am expectant mother—not showing yet—here for my first ultrasound. I am med-student-slash-paramour of the married specialist up on three. I am so-far-survivor combating a malignant intracranial tumor that has enveloped my skull, having already lasted a year and some months past my bleak prognosis. I am loyal offspring, weekly caller to a disintegrating father who, some days, remembers my name.

An improvement from when everyone knows exactly who you are. When you wear slippers to dinner and aren't allowed to ride the elevators.

I am small woman passing through automatic sliding doors Thursday after Thursday to be not no one.

*

Back at my apartment house, I realize my watch battery has died. I check my empty mailbox to make sure my neighbors haven't left anything behind and see

3B approaching.

Excuse me, do you have the time?

"Fine, thanks." Her eyes sweeping the floor. That pinch of skin between plucked bare brows.

And she's outside, pulling her jacket closer around herself. Perhaps staving off some chill she's just walked through.

Through the lobby window I watch her turn out of sight toward the garage, and then I begin climbing upward. I pause mid-flight, something alive and winged shuddering suddenly in the pit of my stomach, colors sharpening, shifting to surreal intensities, the slow sound of footfalls ascending carpeted stairs escalating my pulse, the shadowed image of a hand sliding silently up a polished banister pinning my feet to the floor. But the dim staircase below me is empty. No one comes.

Once my paralysis breaks, I scurry to my apartment and, like a frightened child, crawl beneath my bed frame, wait for breath to slow, for colors to adjust back to normal. Then I crawl back out and defrost dinner.

*

Attempt 1—Bargain carpet reeks of cheap spilled beer, weed,

and feet. Wrist-warmth flows dark as floormates shriek

laughter from the hallway. A girl on the floor behind

a locked door, slipping consciousness, like falling

asleep, limbs losing feeling, numb acceptance

of this romantic ideal that some of us

are meant to die young.

*

Wanting to die is not a disorder.

My therapist disagrees, however, and instead we speak about the anxieties of climbing, the ghost mounting ever closer, steady tread upon carpeted stairs, the shadowed hand gliding upward over smoothed wood.

I sleep with a man who shares my cab one Thursday. A clerk at the law firm down the block from the hospital, he hails a taxi as rain tries not to fall. A co-incidence, his working late and my shift having just ended volunteering on the terminal children's floor.

The driver lets us out at a bar, the clerk paying my share of the fare. He holds the door for me and watches my ass as I enter before him.

With the exception of the bartender, a haggard woman probably in her fifties, and the few sporadic patrons sitting several stools apart at the bar, the room is empty, some country tune the only sound crooning from the jukebox. Cigarette smoke hovers, unmoving, over the bar like an aura that claims the place though, for the life of me, I can't identify a lit cigarette anywhere.

"Here?" the clerk asks, gesturing to a corner table under a burnt-out light bulb that hangs naked from the ceiling.

I smile and let him hold the back of the chair as I scoot into place. He's not unattractive, glasses unable to subdue almost violet eyes, a ghost of acne that occasionally plagues the best of us even into our thirties, dark hair in disarray after a long day of arguing the bottom line with people who paid someone else to make their problems disappear.

"Wha'can I getcha, honey?" The bartender steps to our table, lighting a cigarette off a leopard print lighter and never makes eye contact. The clerk gestures in my direction. I tell her my order and inspect the purple paint on her lips as she sucks on her cigarette and try to imagine the color on my mother but can't.

*

In my own bed with a stranger's thigh swung heavily over my stomach, I pretend not to hear the awful shufflings that seem to be coming from the fire escape out my open bedroom window. I concentrate on the clockwork snores from my companion, the ascent and drop of his chest, but can't dispel from my mind the image of grease-blackened fingers prying stiffly at iron stairs, a bloated body dragging behind, bitter breath clouding chilled air, work boots squeaking slightly as they slide over the crest of yet another stair, another,

another,

shadowed bulk creeping, one step at a time, ever closer to my window sill.

I wait wide-eyed until just after dawn, wanting to crawl under the bed, when the clerk stirs awake, startled undoubtedly by his own breathing, and crawls quietly out of bed. I shut my eyes as he pulls his pants from the floor and tiptoes toward the hallway.

I pretend I'm asleep to be not abandoned.

*

Attempt 2—Fire snuffs itself somewhere between bathroom

and bedroom. Disconnected smoke detector winks,

amused, its battery depleted. Twenty-something

wakes at three the next afternoon with a sore

throat, vodka-valium headache, and

a dusting of ash to sweep away.

*

My therapist speaks in terms of dreams and symbolism even though I swear I am awake. Fears of progress, of dreams realized, he says, feelings of entrapment. We disagree.

"What exactly do you want out of these sessions?"

to be fucking...

to be n o t s o ...

Tongue suddenly voids all predictable clichés.

to be n o t s o ...

A pen keeps tapping. A deep line sewn between bushy brows. "What?"

*

My father's descent into hell was a quick one—a bourbon plunge down basement stairs. Already orphaned by a mother lost years before when "*kee*" and
"*mo*" and "*thair*" and "*pee*" were funny sounds that must have fit some tune. Her
fingers, bone gray and unshaking, trace a dry path down my cheek.

*

Attempt 3—Third time's charm slips, heavy, through the cracked
link of broken chain, hits the floor with a fist. Garage door
yawns awake. Smoke starts to clear. Concerned neighbor
stands not two feet away, calls answering machine from
his cell to say, "You left your car running. I'll grab
your key and leave it in your mailbox."
Inside, a woman wilting behind
tempered glass.

*

The sound of footfalls ascends carpeted stairs; the shadowed image of a father's
hand slides silently up a polished banister.

I am young girl hiding underbed, scissors in hand, lopping off fistfuls of hair to
be not "sweet girl," but ghost girl.

*

In the lobby, 3B drops her gaze to the floor and hurries past me when we cross.
To be not paranoid, I call up the retreating stairwell for her to have a good night
and step back from the chair's edge, desperation's knot a lump at my throat.

I pull my own jacket closer around myself as I step out into heavy air and shiver,
even though I am the chill. Facing forward as I move away from the building,
I pretend not to feel their eyes on me, the drapes tugged back just enough to
notice, blinds pried apart and peered through, their whispered voices.

"…she's the one…"

"…h e r…"

"...the one 5E found in her car...cheeks flushing pink...lips red...sipping in poisoned air...exhaust fogging the garage..."

I pretend not to think about footfalls on carpeted stairs, the garage door groaning awake, purple wrist scars, elevators that rumble through walls at night but don't stop. I pretend not to think about my mother's finger on my face, 5E stretching, reaching for the key in the ignition, chasing valium with vodka with vodka with valium, a match hissing, sparking to life, and the elevators don't stop, my father, the shadow at my bedroom door, and that hand sliding up, up.

I fight the urge to spin toward them, safe behind their own panes of glass, to validate the gnawing sting of paranoia prickling at the back of my neck, and I walk.

In the harsh daylight that is Thursday afternoon, grief falls away. Grievances are atoned for. To be not afraid, I face forward and walk on, ignoring the faces behind the panes, the whispered truths I feel creeping close, close behind me. Dead stay buried where they land at the bottom. Therapeutic salvation battles insecurity and dead men scaling basement stairs.

Something About the Birds

Spring.

We moved into this neighborhood over two months ago, and it won't stop raining. Our house, a neo-mansard two-story with a half-finished, walk-out basement. A sprawling floor plan, three bedrooms, three-and-a-half baths, abundant livable as well as storage space. The back lot of the property slopes into a wooded jungle of green, especially vibrant under all of this rain. The front windows face a quiet suburban street, no sidewalks, so, on rare rainless days, the neighbors' kids pedal their first two-wheelers down the middle of the road, careen wide arcs up our driveway, and roll back out onto black asphalt where drivers know to slow their speed and stay vigilant. We're the last house before the cusp of a cul-de-sac, so traffic mostly belongs to our street save the occasional delivery truck.

Neighbors wave to each other here, a quick raise of the palm driving or walking past. Even as I read in my main level study beside the water-strewn window, they catch me through the pane, lift a hand in greeting from the street. This reminds me of the *boaters' code*, summers ago on our twenty-five foot cuddy cabin cutting through brown breakers on the Illinois River, except minus the seedy swinger rumors that surrounded our mainly middle-aged marina. Passing boats often brandished as many as ten palms extended in simultaneous greeting, and Peter and I would comply in form, feeling funny about it but wanting to fit in, not wanting to stand out as rude or seemingly superior to our older and sometimes flirtatious cohorts. We sold the boat two summers ago as repair costs exceeded what we paid for our slip and for gas the few times a season we were able to cast off. This was around the same time we began house-hunting, hoping for a place away from our city street apartment where the perpetual sounds of sirens wailed into the early morning, where I kept an aluminum baseball bat next to the bed, where walking to my car in the back lot invited harassment and pleas for pocket change.

Peter and I aren't married, though most strangers assume we are. We've been together thirteen years, lived together nine. We engage in self- and other-deprecating banter; we enjoy each other's company, hold hands in public, grocery shop as a pair, sometimes retreat to separate stations when bored or peeved at the other, but always under the same roof, him to his workbench in the basement, me to the study on the main level. We'd like one day to make a family.

The small balcony off the upstairs master bedroom is rotting and in need of sealing, and rain drips into the living room into a garbage can I've positioned in front of the couch. Water also seeps in at the foundation in the basement, though fortunately this has been restricted to the unfinished area where we've stacked cardboard boxes and plastic bins up on pallets a few inches off the concrete.

We're not married because Peter doesn't believe a slip of paper should determine a relationship status and because his own family was cracked in half by parental divorce, his two older brothers departing with their father, Peter and his sister left behind with their mother. He references the mutual contempt, the pitting of child against parent, the guilt trips over visits, the alimony disputes, the custody hearings, the forced therapy sessions. His siblings are all on their first marriage; all have children. Nonetheless, his faith in the institution is shaken, and no amount of emotional discussion or contrary evidence sways him.

One overcast but dry afternoon, I circle the perimeter of the house to check the progress of the seeds and bulbs I planted our first week here. The house stands out from the neighbors' in that, with the exception of the lush forest behind the property, the lot is devoid of vegetation. The front yard is a flat expanse of grass, treeless, flowerless, no shrubs, buds, or blossoms of any sort, siding and large panes of glass fully exposed to the street. One of our neighbors, a dad from down the street, told us that a bachelor lived in our house for years before we moved in, a night shift factory lineman who showed no interest in maintaining a picturesque façade. I take on the reversal of this trend as my personal mission.

Nothing grows yet. I glance up into the sunless sky, wish for change, for light and warmth. The woman from across the street, a young mother pushing her twins in a stroller along the curb, raises her hand in greeting, and I return the gesture. Beyond her relaxed pace, her front yard blooms in color as tulips open in bright reds and yellows; a pear tree bursts white petals.

I circle to the back of our house, find a cardinal, its neck broken, a puddle of red feathers on the patio stone. I'm not good at this type of thing, but I find a gardening shovel, scoop the little body up, and pitch it down the sloped earth, into the woods. A drizzle starts to fall, so I go back inside, read by the rain-streaked study window. In the street outside, minivans and SUVs splash rainwater up over curbs, parents bringing their kids home from school. Several who notice me at the window lift a hand in acknowledgement.

Summer.

Cardinals keep slamming into the back windows. Peter reads on the internet that it's a territorial thing, that they should stop once breeding season has ended. I find their dead bodies on the patio stone, red-feathered necks twisted, toss them with my shovel down the slope, into the trees. Soon after, the clockwork thwaps as another one thinks he's warding away competition when it's his own muted reflection in the glass. I smooth some static clings over the pane—snow-flakes in June, but it's all I have—to clear up the confusion, but within days, I go outside to water the soil and find its small corpse, a red heap at my feet.

And my plants aren't growing. The gardens I started lie empty, vacant beds of dirt and dust. The rain has stopped, the drought begun, and as often as I circle the perimeter of the house with my watering can, the little seedlings that have sprouted up and out from the soil wilt, give up, and die. I don't know enough about under-watering and over-watering, so I try both, fail. Outside the back windows, lush greenery; out the front windows are other people's children splashing in kiddie pools, dancing through sprinklers, racing bikes, pushed in strollers, pulled in wagons. Their parents with the mechanical waves.

Peter's sister visits with her family, insists on staying in a hotel so the children don't dishevel our house with their toys and their temper-tantrums. Plus, she says, it's not as though we've child-proofed the place. The kids call me "auntie" even though technically, legally, I am not. As their parents and Peter sit outside at the hotel pool, I read the children stories, tuck them carefully into bed for their naps, kiss their sleeping faces. And I feel empty inside, scraped out, hollow.

At home, the front lawn is browning under the naked gaze of the sun. I keep watering, but to no avail. Nothing grows here.

Peter and I argue more, the frustration of things not going as planned, of failed attempts. Long, barren stretches of silence. We withdraw more often to separate corners, him to the basement, me to my books, my dead gardens. And the birds keep committing suicide.

Despite the sweltering temperatures, I always feel cold, spend more time outside. I water the soil, the dying grass, position my lounger under the sun to warm my skin, to chase the shivering chill away. Neighbors walk past, women guiding strollers in tandem, a moms' club I'm not a part of. They see me and wave in unison without a smile or disruption of their mom-speak, walk away, their little ones lethargic and sweating under cloth canopies. I pretend to read, to focus on the pages in front of me, but I watch the families shrink into the landscape of the neighborhood, lawns lined with hedges and crowded by flowerbeds, shaded by flourishing branches which dangle tire swings, leaves which rustle and whisper gossip in the hot breeze. And I feel so alone.

I let the sun scorch my skin. My insides, I think, must be ash. When the red blisters begin to peel, Peter calls me irresponsible, and I strip the outer layer away, crave new beginnings.

For the most part, the inside of the house has shaped up nicely. A fresh coat of paint in the living room, the wood of the master balcony replaced and watertight, new plush carpeting in the basement. I arrange cut flowers bought at the grocery store in vases across the main floor, pockets of color that remind me to hope, on coffee tables and end tables, on tiered stands, on kitchen counters, centered on our little dinette set for two. The second and third bedrooms we initially left empty, anticipating new furniture, a future, we now crowd with boxes, stash things we haven't decided to save or throw away, and the doors stay closed.

Peter works tirelessly on the outside of the house, replacing rotted wood around windows, patching the roof, touching up paint where necessary. I tend to the dry cracked dirt in the gardens, watering until mud bubbles and pools up, spills over onto the driveway. Then I water the lawn, hose water raining down, straw-like blades crunching under my feet. I round the corner to the backyard to find Peter who measures deck boards in the shade of intertwining maple branches. My presence startles away a cardinal who has just begun to thump against the patio windows. The bird flutters off into the woods, a red speck swallowed by green where the rattle of cicadas suddenly intensifies, crescendos into an unnerving roar before just as suddenly it ceases.

Fall.

Up and down our street, trees bleed leaves onto lawns. The road is a winding trail of red, orange, and gold confetti, someone else's parade having just passed through. Our yard is bare. The woods behind us briefly transformed into a brilliant yellow out the back windows before quickly shedding their colors one overnight, and we woke to bony blackened branches, stark naked and empty.

I sit and read by the study windows. The family of five across the street shares the task of raking and bagging leaves. They work as a smooth-running machine, moving in unison, each clearing a separate patch of grass, orange jack-o-lantern trash bag stretched wide and smiling, ready for a full load of leaves lifted on an upturned rake, each team member seeming attuned to the others without obvious verbal communication. One of the little boys catches me watching and waves, which sparks four other gloved hands to rise into the air. I wave back, move away from the window, bump up the temperature on the thermostat to kick the furnace on. I'm always so cold.

Peter has begun to spend Sunday afternoons at a bar across town with cowork- ers. I've started a book club with some of my women friends and tried to orga- nize it to overlap with his absences, so that we could meet during those hours I spend alone. However, my friends have husbands and kids, and Sunday after- noons away from home are off limits. As are evenings and weekend hours in general. Our meeting time is still up in the air.

I plant some Rose of Sharon along the driveway, hope that next spring the small bushes will sprout. I drag a rake to the back yard, the only area where leaves, brown and decomposing, litter the grass and require removal. Scratching at the ground with metal hooks, I clear the space around me in sweeping arcs while the gaunt trees with their black bark weave and sway in the wind, bend treach- erously close to the powerlines. I shiver against the chill, move away from the house, closer to where the earth slopes away, the hooks of my rake tangling in the dry leaves, in the grass.

Buried in the browning foliage near the base of a tree trunk, I find a fallen nest. Four eggs lie inside, one cracked open, holding the pink hued body of a baby cardinal. I let the rake slip to the ground and reach with gloved hands for the little abandoned nest.

Down in the hollow of the trees, where our property drops off, falls away, disembodied voices of children echo and cry, and I can't tell where they're coming from or where they're going, and I think they must be ghosts, dim, dead children playing chase in the shadows. I don't know where to go from here, so I'm still, listless and listening, pining for the ghost babies lost in the trees, clutching the rotting nest with the bad eggs inside.

Winter.

Acknowledgments

"Scattershot" originally appeared in *Bluffs Literary Magazine*

"Brick" originally appeared in *Heart* journal

"Something About the Birds" originally appeared in *Festival Writer*